THE GUARDIANS *of* GA'HOOLE

Book One: *The Capture*

Book Two: *The Journey*

Book Three: *The Rescue*

Book Four: *The Siege*

Book Five: *The Shattering*

Book Six: *The Burning*

Book Seven: *The Hatchling*

Book Eight: *The Outcast*

Book Nine: *The First Collier*

Book Ten: *The Coming of Hoole*

Book Eleven: *To Be a King*

Book Twelve: *The Golden Tree*

Book Thirteen: *The River of Wind*

Book Fourteen: *Exile*

Book Fifteen: *The War of the Ember*

*A Guide Book to the Great Tree*

*Lost Tales of Ga'Hoole*

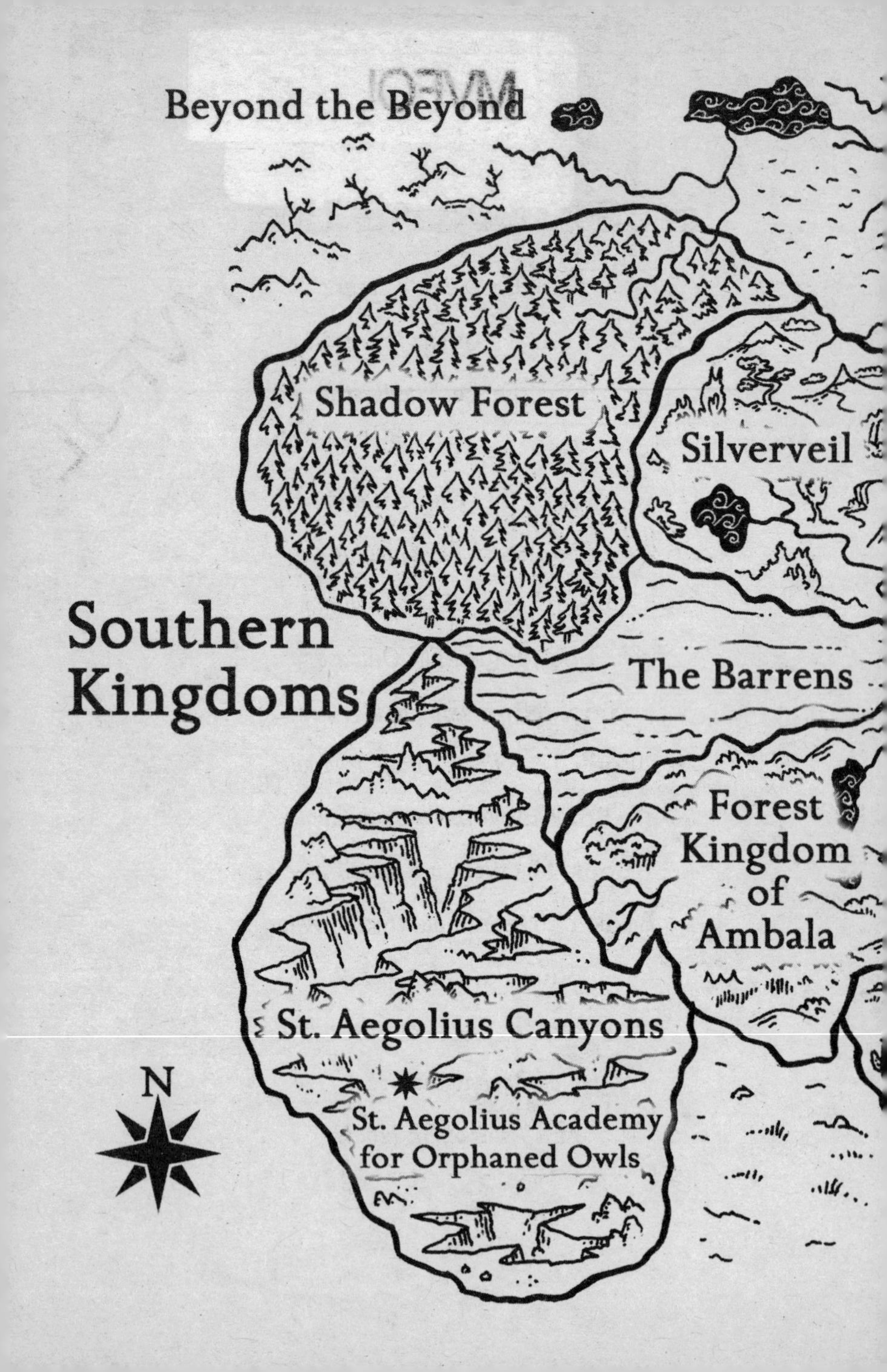
Beyond the Beyond
Shadow Forest
Silverveil
Southern Kingdoms
The Barrens
Forest Kingdom of Ambala
St. Aegolius Canyons
St. Aegolius Academy for Orphaned Owls
N

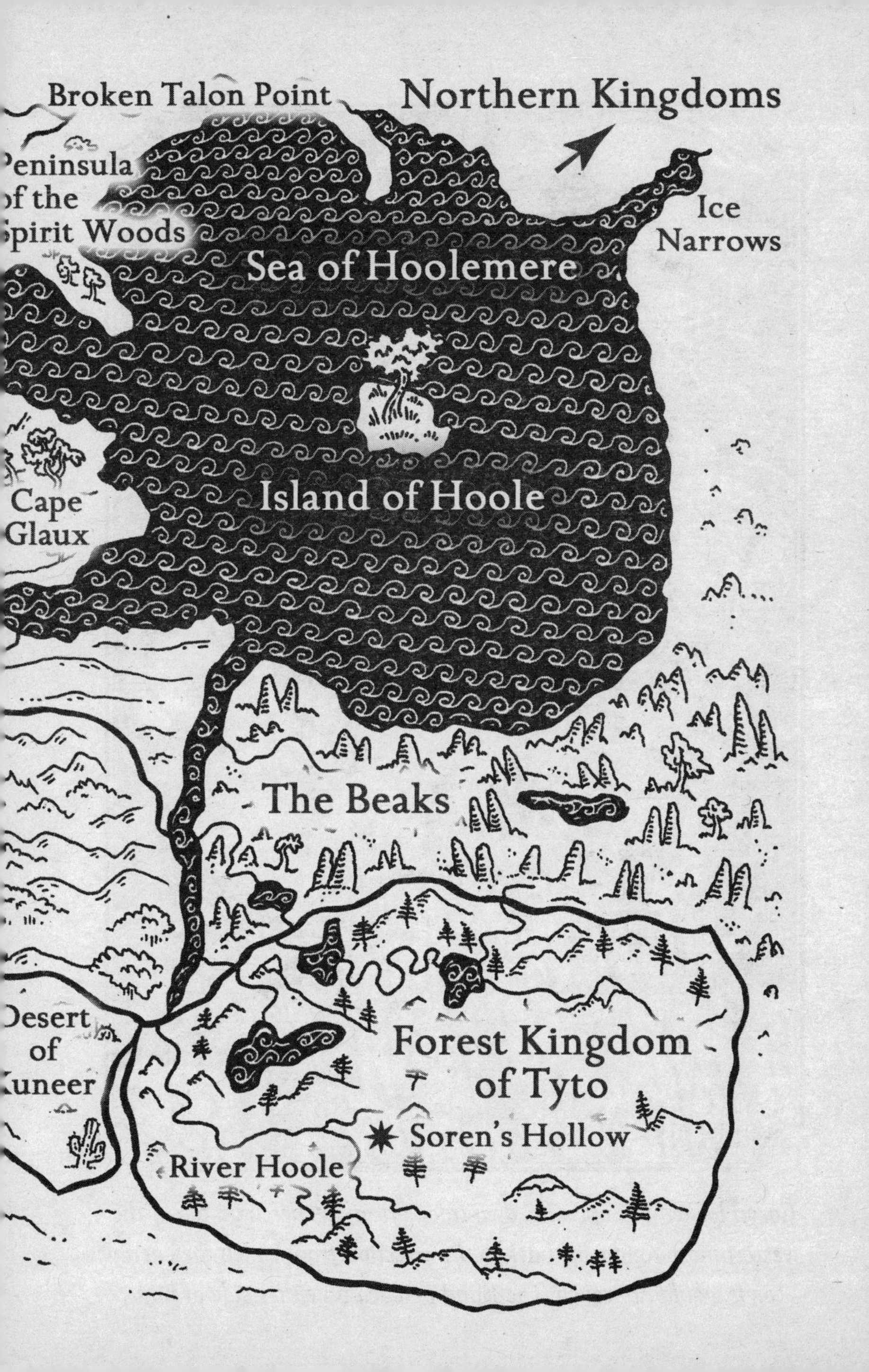
Broken Talon Point
Northern Kingdoms
Peninsula
f the
pirit Woods
Ice
Narrows
Sea of Hoolemere
Island of Hoole
Cape
Glaux
The Beaks
Desert
of
uneer
Forest Kingdom
of Tyto
Soren's Hollow
River Hoole

*Coryn looked out upon his own troops from his perch on top of the westernmost Yondo, his back to the direction from which the enemy owls would approach. The Band perched on either side of him.*

# GUARDIANS of GA'HOOLE

BOOK FIFTEEN

# *The War of the Ember*

BY KATHRYN LASKY

SCHOLASTIC INC.

New York Toronto London Auckland
Sydney Mexico City New Delhi Hong Kong

ISBN 978-0-439-88809-7



Artwork by Richard Cowdrey
Design by Steve Scott

12 11 10 9 8 12 13 14 15/0

Printed in the U.S.A. 40

First printing, November 2008

*I dedicate this book to all of you Guardians of Ga'Hoole readers who have become like citizens in my imaginary world. Imagination is, in a sense, a two-way street. Through your enthusiasm you have made this world much more real for me. I had originally intended to write only six books. This book, the fifteenth, is the last. It is the last not because your fervor has waned but because this is the logical place for the story of Soren and the Band to conclude.*

*–KL*

# Northern Kingdoms

Glauxian Brothers Retreat

Bitter Sea

Kiel Bay

Stormfast Island

Bay of Fangs

Everwinter Sea

Ice Talons

Ice Narrows

Dark Fowl Island

Southern Kingdoms

# Contents

# *Prologue*

*The light of the low-hanging full-shine moon slipped into the cave, making it glow like a lantern of ice above that tiny gut of sea linking the Southern Kingdoms to the Northern Kingdoms. Inside the cave, the shadows of two owls were printed against the radiance of its walls. Was the little puffin imagining it, or did one of those owls have a peculiar tinge, a color like the day sky? Ever since he had found that sky-colored feather he had been obsessed with it.* I'm just seeing sky color everywhere, that's all. I shouldn't be here. I shouldn't be here! I shouldn't be here. *The words coursed through the puffin's head with a monotonous but persistent rhythm.* I am the youngest in a long line of exceedingly stupid birds, *he reminded himself silently as he wedged himself more tightly into his hiding place.* I wish I could grow thinner, *he thought,* like the owls do when they get scared. *He had stuffed his rather plump body into a narrow crevice in the wall at the very back of the cave, in the shadows, where the moonlight could not reach. It was not the most comfortable situation.*

*Little Dumpy, who would be Dumpy the Fifteenth if puffins could count, sensed that what was transpiring in this cave between the two owls was dangerous.* I am not supposed to be here. I'm not sure how I know that this is dangerous but I do. I'm not *that* stupid!

*No, Dumpy was not stupid at all in comparison to the rest of the puffins of the Ice Narrows. Puffins, by and large, thought about only one thing — fishing. They were expert divers and could plunge boldly and accurately into tumultuous waters, returning with a dozen or more capelin neatly lined up in their stubby bright orange beaks to feed their young chicks. But this was about as efficient and precise as puffins ever got. They were generally reckless fliers, and went about the rearing of their young and other matters of the nest in a most haphazard way. When Dumpy had found the sky-colored feather, his siblings and even his parents insisted it was actually white, because they knew the names of no other colors except white and black, the color of their feathers, and orange, the color of their beaks. Therefore no other colors existed in their tiny puffin minds. But Dumpy the Fifteenth's tiny mind, through some quirk of nature, was often crowded with unusual thoughts. Perhaps it had stretched from being so crammed with these odd thoughts. And he knew this feather was not black or orange. And he knew it was* not *white. He simply called it sky.*

*Owls on occasion flew through the Ice Narrows, but Dumpy had never before seen an owl with feathers this color, and when he came across it he had hoped that someday he might find the rest of the owl to whom it belonged. Now the sky-colored owl was before him, and Dumpy was frightened.*

*Dumpy knew of a back tunnel into this cave in the high cliffs of the Narrows and when he had seen the two owls duck into the cave he went around the back just to have a peek. Crushed in this terribly uncomfortable hiding place, he listened. And right now it was not the sky-feathered owl that frightened him but the other one. He guessed it was a Barn Owl but he could not see its face. He supposed it was a female, for it was fairly large and the females usually were larger. That much he knew. This owl had just hung something metal on a spur of ice. Not battle claws. Dumpy had seen battle claws. This metal would not fit on talons. The owl now turned. Dumpy's heart stood still. The full-shine moon falling into the ice cave lit the Barn Owl's face. Glowering, pitted, and scarred, it was not a face but a landscape — a landscape of incredible violence. Featherless in patches, the skin on the left side was puckered here and there into dark red bubbles of flesh. Her eyes glared darkly. A scar slashed down across the devastation of her face.*

*"So now you see me." The Barn Owl spoke to the sky-colored owl in a ragged voice that seemed as torn as her face. "I don't frighten you?"*

*"Madame, yours is a face of glory, of valor. Your face inspires."*

*"Mind you, I don't try to hide it. After the battle in the sixth kingdom, I decided to wear the mask as a tribute to my dead*

*mate, Kludd. It was forged from the remnants of the very one he once wore."*

*She stepped up closer to the sky-feathered owl and flipped her head so that it was almost upside down, and her eyes now captured the reflection of the full-shine moon so that they were no longer black at all, but loomed like two tiny moons within the ravaged landscape of the cratered face.*

*This creature no longer even looked like an owl, let alone a Barn Owl. Dumpy's guts were in turmoil. Nausea swelled in his gullet, as if the capelin fish he had eaten earlier were swimming back up from his stomach. He clamped his beak shut. This was not the time to throw up!*

*"I think, dear Striga, we might be able, you and I, to do business."*

*"I agree, madam."*

*"Madame General," the Barn Owl corrected.*

*"Yes, Madame General, I think that we can do business. I know a great deal about the ember you seek."*

*"Yes . . . yes . . . of course," she replied slowly, "but tell me what you know about hagsfiends."*

Hagsfiends! *The very word sent a horrific shock through Dumpy's body.* Hagsfiends, I've heard that word somewhere, someplace. No! *the puffin corrected himself.* Not heard it, but *knew* it somehow! *Deep within him — Dumpy closed his eyes, trying to remember — there was a dim recollection, a feeling from a time before his time, if that were possible, of an ancient terror. A terror that might have had its very source here in the Ice Narrows, perhaps in this very cave. When he opened his eyes, he saw that the sky-colored owl had wilfed.*

*"Now why have you wilfed on me like that?" the Barn Owl snapped. She flipped her head back to its normal position.*

*"Hagsfiends vanished nearly one thousand years ago," the blue owl said.*

*"And you think they are gone forever?"*

*"Madame General, what are you suggesting?"*

*"I am suggesting that nothing is forever."*

*"Please speak plainly, Madame General. I am no good at riddles."*

*"In three moon cycles."*

*"In three moon cycles, what?"*

*"It will be Long Night, and a marvelous hatching will occur."*

*"There is an egg?"*

Hagsfiends? Eggs? That can't be good, *Dumpy thought.* It could mean more hagsfiends. Isn't that what "eggs" mean? More chicks?

*Nyra cocked her head. Her eyes glinted darkly. "Not yet. But soon." She paused, then continued. "You are not the only one who found cracks in the Panqua Palace. How should I put it? There are servants who can be suborned, and dragon owls who have begun to question their pampered existence. Remember, I was taken for dead after the battle in which you helped defeat my forces. I was badly wounded. I had to recover someplace."*

*"Not the Panqua Palace!"*

*"Yes. Are you surprised? It's large. There are secret chambers, dark corners, hidey-holes. But most important, there were restless owls there. Owls like you, who chafed under their routine of useless luxury. You see, Striga, you are now known on both sides of the River of Wind. As Orlando of the Middle Kingdom, you are the dragon owl who learned to fly — the first in a thousand years. You are an inspiration to the other long-feathered owls eager to break the gilded chains that bind them, other blue owls eager for power!"*

*There was much that Dumpy did not understand in the conversation that he had just heard. But there were two things that he did understand: The name of the color of this owl was "blue," not "sky," and something terrible was coming to his world — and not just to the Ice Narrows but to the kingdoms they linked, and perhaps far beyond!*

## CHAPTER ONE

# The Harvest Festival

*Dearest tree, we give our thanks*
*For your blessings through the years.*
*Vines heavy with sweet berries*
*Nourish us and quench our fears.*

*And in times of summer drought,*
*Searing heat or winter's cold,*
*From your bounty freely given*
*We grow strong and we grow bold.*

*Let us always tend with care*
*Your bark, your roots, your vines so fair.*

Soren and Pelli stood on the balcony with Bell and Bash, trembling with joy as they watched Blythe singing to the accompaniment of the grass harp.

"Mum, she is really good!" Bell said, her voice drenched in wonder at her sister's accomplishments.

"And you should hear her when she sings one of those old gadfeather songs," Bash exclaimed.

"Hymns don't really do her voice justice," Gylfie said. And no sooner was the hymn completed than there was a loud twang as Mrs. Plithiver jumped the strings over an octave. "Oh, here it comes!" Gylfie exclaimed. "She's going to sing that old gadfeather gizzard-acher!"

*When an owl loves an owl*
*And your gizzard's about to break,*
*Let me tell you, you can't do nothin'*
*'Cept to follow in that wake.*
*Don't turn tail, just go on. . . .*

Halfway through the song, Soren and Pelli turned to each other. Their black eyes were bright with a mixture of joy and alarm. "Great Glaux!" Soren exclaimed. "Do you think she's courting already?"

"Oh, Da!" Bell and Bash both said at the same time.

"It's just an old gadfeather love song," Bell said.

"With a little R and H beat laid in to make it more modern," Bash added.

Pelli blinked. "What in Glaux's name is R and H?"

"Rhythm and hoots," Bell said. "And not everybody can sing it. It's complicated, and Blythe is great, and Mrs. P. said that because of Blythe the harp guild snakes have developed a whole new style of plucking."

Soren and Pelli exchanged glances. Their eyes glistened with unshed tears as they gazed at Bell, her sister Blythe's staunchest fan. But a year before, under the powerful, malignant influence of the Striga, Bell had tried to discourage her sister from singing. Bell had believed, as the Striga had told her, that singing, along with many other artistic and playful pursuits that owls of the great tree had enjoyed, was a "vanity," a word now rarely heard around the Great Ga'Hoole Tree without causing a shiver deep in one's gizzard.

The Striga, this peculiar blue owl from the sixth kingdom, had saved Bell's life, and Coryn's and the Band's, as well, for he had learned of a plan to assassinate them. By saving them, the Striga had earned the deepest gratitude of the owls of the Great Ga'Hoole Tree. Little did anyone suspect that this tattered, blue-feathered owl would become a terrible danger. On Balefire Night, one of the most joyous holidays of the owl year, the Striga had finally been driven from the tree. Now singing, and all else the Striga had forbidden as vanity, was once again welcome at the tree. Blythe was singing her gizzard out and no one was happier than Bell.

"Look at Otulissa and Cleve!" Pelli exclaimed. Cleve had put his wing gently around Otulissa and was crooning softly in her ear slit. From watching his beak, Soren could see that Cleve was repeating the last words of the gadfeather song. Soren had to stifle a churr as it seemed so improbable that anyone could get away with crooning anything to Otulissa. But Cleve was another story. There had never been two owls more different from each other than Cleve and Otulissa. Cleve of Firthmore was a prince from an ancient dynastic line of owls in the Northern Kingdoms who had given up his title and inheritance to pursue a meditative life studying the healing arts at the Glauxian Brothers retreat. He was also a dedicated gizzard-resister. He would not fight nor would he fly with battle claws. Otulissa, although she shared his scholarly nature, was a seasoned warrior. She commanded the Strix Struma Strikers. Could a dedicated soldier and a gizzard-resister find true happiness together? Apparently they could.

Gylfie noticed Soren observing Cleve. "I would say that Blythe is singing their song."

"If it hadn't been for Cleve," Pelli said, "I don't think

Otulissa would have ever taken wing again. She would have just retreated into her books."

"Out of the way! Out of the way!" Fritha, a young Pygmy Owl barreled through the birds that had crowded the balcony. "I've got to go to press. I have to include a review of this concert in the next edition. Your sister was great!" she shouted to Bell as she flew by.

"I'll help!" Bell called out, and flew after her. "I'll make sure you get all the details right."

Soren, the rest of the Band, and Coryn enjoyed the night air in silence a moment on a branch just outside of the Great Hollow. The dancing had begun.

"Quite a difference from last year," Coryn said. The Band seemed relieved that Coryn had said what was in everyone's mind — that last year Coryn had been so completely duped by the Striga that the tree had nearly been lost to that fanatical blue owl and his converts. Left unsaid, it would have hung like the last vaporous shreds of a dark storm cloud. The evening, however, was lovely, the air smooth for dancing.

"The dancing will go on late," Gylfie said.

"Good!" Coryn exclaimed with unbridled joy. "Good!"

By the time dawn broke, the first edition of *The Evening Hoot* was completed. The owls, tipsy from the milkberry wine or from dancing the glauc-glauc, had long since staggered to their hollows. They would be able to read *The Hoot* that evening at tweener. The headline screamed HARVEST FESTIVAL BACK IN FULL FORCE: STUNNING SINGING DEBUT! B FLAT? NO WAY!

> *Blythe, one of the three daughters of Soren and Pelli, opened the Harvest Festival celebration with the traditional "Dearest Tree" carol. Singing with clarity and lovely expression, she gave a polished rendition of that beloved song. However, it was when young Blythe broke into her next number, an old gadfeather favorite, that we saw what a daring artist this little owl is. Belting out "When an Owl Loves an Owl," she was all gizzard!*
>
> *There was obvious musical chemistry between Blythe and the members of the harp guild, in particular with the brilliant Mrs. Plithiver, who gyrated through those strings, twanging and plucking in her capacity as a sliptween with unmatched precision. After last year's disastrous festival, this reporter cannot imagine a better way to commence the harvest celebration than with this bold, self-assured young singer and the brilliant sliptween.*

# CHAPTER TWO

# Dumpy's Dilemma

The moonlight in the ice cave had grown faint. It had felt like forever before the two owls left. Their conversation had sent chills through Dumpy, and for a bird hatched and reared in the Ice Narrows to feel chilly was freakish. And what was that word the owl had said? *Hagsfiend!* It sounded frightening. And then Dumpy realized that the crevice he was lodged in had suddenly become roomier; that a thing he thought could never happen had happened. *I've wilfed. Actually wilfed. I've grown skinny with fear. Owls wilf, not puffins! Oh, dear . . . oh, dear. I must REALLY be scared. What are these hagsfiends the owls spoke of? And what does their talk of "eggs" mean?* Dumpy's head almost ached as he felt his brain stretching as it never had before. Little slivers of thought, sharp as ice needles when the katabats blew, were storming through his mind.

*What is the meaning of all I have seen and heard here?*

Dumpy tried to recall his second-to-last thought before the mind storm in his wee brain had begun.

*I must* do *something! And that scares me almost as much as what I have seen and heard. I must* do *something! But what?*

Then Dumpy the Fifteenth's thoughts came swiftly. *I must tell someone what I have heard and seen. Not Pop and Mummy. They're too stupid. Grandpop and Grummy — even stupider!* He thought of his older brother, the Chubster. *No, never! Oh, Great Ice, what am I to do?* Then it came to him. *I must tell somebody smart. Should I go to the Great Ga'Hoole Tree? The owls! The Guardians!* He'd seen them once or twice. And there were the four called the Band. *Oh, and that very nice Spotted Owl from the north. What was his name?... Cluck, Clem — Cleve! Yes, Cleve.* Cleve had passed through when Dumpy was just a chick. But he remembered. Indeed, he did! Dumpy's foot had had a sea tick lodged in it, and Cleve had removed it. *I must find Cleve and I must find the Band. But they're so smart, and I'm so dumb! It would be so embarrassing, and it's so far to travel. Maybe... maybe I can tell the polar bears. They are big and tough. And they're much closer.*

Dumpy waddled to the back entrance of the cliff cave and perched on a ledge that overhung the Ice Narrows. He looked down into the churning waters. He could see his brother, the Chubster, as he was known, diving for fish for his own young family. The Chubster caught sight of him, opened his beak to shout a greeting, and the twenty-four fish that he had neatly lined up in his beak dropped back into the sea.

"Ah, for the love of ice!" A squawk erupted from one of the ice nests that notched the cliffs. "Chub, you idiot. You lost our dinner!" It was the Chubster's mate, Pulkie.

"Just wanted to say hi to Dumpy. Hey, Dumpster, baby! How's it icing?"

"I got young'uns to feed," Pulkie shouted, and blasted out of the nest. Folding her wings back against her plump sides, she hurled herself into the thrashing water below. Some baby pufflings peered over the edge of the ice nest.

The Chubster, oblivious to his hungry pufflings, flew up to where Dumpy perched. "What 'cha doing?"

"Uh . . . nothing." Dumpy wasn't sure if he should say anything to his brother about what he had just witnessed. He tried changing the subject. "Pulkie — she can really dive. Look at her."

"Yep, she's a can-do sort of puffin. You got to get yourself a mate, Dumpy."

"I don't think I'm ready."

"Ready? Mum always said you were the smartest. Too smart for your own good maybe."

Dumpy blinked. *She might be right,* he thought. "Uh . . . listen, I got to go."

"Go where?" asked the Chubster.

"I'm not sure," Dumpy said.

"Imnotsure! A fabulous place!" the Chubster exclaimed. "Heard all about it. Great fishing."

"Uh, well, I better be off." Dumpy spread his wings and lifted off the edge of the cliff. He heard the Chubster yelling at his pufflings. "Wave bye-bye to Uncle Dumpy. He's going to Imnotsure."

Pulkie was back in the ice nest, sorting fish. She and the pufflings turned and looked wistfully at Dumpy as he dissolved into the fog bank over the Ice Narrows.

*Oh my, fog. Which way do I go?* Dumpy thought. Finally, he carved a turn and headed north toward the end of summer gathering place for the bears. He knew where that was. Not far from the Ice Narrows. But what should he tell them? He tried to order the facts in his disorderly mind. First there was the strange blue owl. And the owl with the frightening face. But worse than what they looked like was what they said. *Hagsfiends.* What were hagsfiends? Another kind of bird? Definitely not a polar bear. The faint dark memory stirred again, like a shadow invading his being.

Dumpy must have been flying faster than he thought, for soon he was looking down at the remnants of summer ice in the Everwinter Sea. He followed the floes up the Firth of Fangs. He hoped the polar bears were still there and had not begun their long swim north to the more remote firths and small channels where they hibernated for the winter. He spiraled down, and to his great delight saw several bears swimming about and some reclining on floes with their cubs. Many of the floes were bloody with freshly killed seals. The polar bears were fattening up for their long winter sleep.

The firth was quite narrow at this point, and Dumpy saw one bear slip off an ice floe and swim toward the base of the cliffs where there appeared to be a cave. Dumpy hovered outside. It was hard to understand these bears, with their thick Krakish accent. Thankfully, many of them spoke a mixture of Hoolian and Krakish, and Dumpy was catching a few words here and there.

"Gunda grunuch and see you in two years . . . Eeh, Sveep?" Then the most enormous head Dumpy had ever seen poked out of the cave and roared in a clear voice. "Svarr, you are about as romantic as a mess of seal guts. Love 'em and leave, huh?"

"Well, mating season doesn't last forever, and I'm getting sleepy. The katabats are blowing early," replied a male bear who was treading water outside the cave.

"You just want to skedaddle."

"Here, I'll get you something to eat before I go." The bear swooped an immense paw through the water and snatched up a large fish. "Bluescale — token of my affection." He slapped it down on the rock ledge by the cave.

"Great Ice!" Dumpy sputtered. The two bears looked up.

"What do you want?" the bears roared.

"That fish — that fish. Never saw one that color. Sky. I mean blue," Dumpy said, alighting on the ice floe the male bear had just vacated. "I saw an owl that color. Blue . . ." Dumpy repeated the word softly, almost as if he were tasting it.

"I'm out of here," Svarr said. "Same time, same place, two years from now." He yawned and began to swim off. "Hope you get some cubs. I'm sure they'll be cute, just like their mum."

The female sighed. "As if he'll ever bother to visit them."

"You mean he'll never see his cubs?" said Dumpy.

"Never."

"That's very sad," Dumpy said. "I mean, he doesn't know what he's missing."

The bear blinked. "What is your name, puffin?"

"Dumpy."

"Well, Dumpy, mine is Sveep, and I think that is very astute of you."

"What's 'astute'?"

"Smart, keen."

Now it was Dumpy's turn to blink. "No . . . no one has ever called me — or any a puffin — smart, keen, or . . . or astute."

"Well, I'm calling you that. Now tell me, what is this about a blue owl?"

Dumpy hoped he could give a halfway intelligible recitation of what he had seen. He began slowly. "There is this cave in the Ice Narrows. Two owls came to it. One had these feathers that you call blue, and the other . . . the other . . ."

When Dumpy had finished the story, Sveep was silent for several seconds, then finally she spoke. "This does not sound good. Not good at all. But it's owl business."

"What should I do?"

"You must seek out the owls," she said. "The Guardians of Ga'Hoole."

Dumpy's head drooped. For a bird that possessed one of the most comical faces, with its bright orange beak and odd facial markings, Dumpy at this moment looked positively tragic. "I can't," he whispered into his breast feathers.

"What do you mean 'you can't'?" Sveep said. She was beginning to feel that seasonal sleepiness that afflicted polar bears at this time of year, when they sensed the first signs of winter, when seconds, then minutes clipped off each day's light. Nonetheless, she fought the lethargy that beckoned her insistently. This was important. "I repeat, why can't you seek the owls?" Her words were becoming thick.

"The Guardians are all so smart. I am so stupid."

This was like of jolt of summer sun through her body. "Nonsense! You're the smartest puffin I've ever met!" she said emphatically.

"Do you mean that?" Dumpy asked.

"I mean it. You have to go."

"I'll . . . I'll think about it!"

"Don't think about it — do it!"

CHAPTER THREE

# Chimes in the Mist

Deep in the Shadow Forest, the darkest of all the forests of the Southern Kingdoms, there was a place where the thickly wooded land dipped suddenly into a cleft in the earth. The depression was hardly noticeable from above because the trees were dense, and mist from a waterfall obscured the land itself. Within this cleft, there was a stone palace left from the time of the Others, and in the palace dwelled a Boreal Owl named Bess. Less than a dozen owls in all the kingdoms knew of this palace or the Boreal Owl. To these owls, the Boreal Owl was not just Bess, but Bess of the Chimes — or the Knower, one of the most learned owls in the six owl kingdoms. To the few owls who knew of this place, it seemed odd that it was called a palace. It was more like a vast library, with books, and maps, and charts, and ancient scientific instruments. Bess herself never left the Palace of Mists. She had arrived years before with the bones of her father, determined to mourn him in the time-honored tradition of Boreal Owls.

On this particular night, she was just finishing her evening ritual. The bones of her father, Grimble, had long since crumbled to dust and blown away, but the place they had lain in the bell tower, beneath the bell, had become a hallowed place for Bess, and every evening at tween time she flew within the confines of the enormous hood of the clapperless bell and sang her song in the chimelike tones unique to Boreal Owls. The last verse always gave her hope that someday she would join her beloved father, Grimble, in glaumora, so she always sang it with a robust spirit.

*Glaux ring in this noble owl,*
*Sound the clapper made of mist.*
*Ting ting, I hear it now.*
*How can a scroom resist*
*This lovely tolling sound,*
*Which calls you from on high?*
*Fly on, dear Da, fly on.*
*Owl angels wait and sigh.*

As she finished the last verse of the song, she sensed a presence near the tower. It would not be the Band.

They knew better than to intrude during her prayers. She settled uneasily on the window ledge of the tower and swiveled her head around. She heard a gasp from a niche in the circular stone wall. A soft violet light suffused the tower, and she thought she saw a lump of feathers in the niche. They billowed, then settled, then billowed again in long intervals. A ragged breath escaped. "Great Glaux!" she whispered to herself and swooped down. She saw on the narrow floor of the niche a Boreal Owl in grave distress. He attempted to lift his head, but it flopped back down.

Bess was stunned. This owl was a stranger. It had been years since a stranger had found its way to the Palace of Mists, let alone a sickly stranger. The intruder spoke.

"I have come . . . to . . . die." The words were delivered in breathy little puffs. "Die beneath the bell."

"But you are alone." Bess said.

"No matter . . . You shall sing me to glaumora, shall you not? I have been poisoned."

"But surely there are antidotes."

"No . . . . The poison is in my gizzard. You shall sing me to glaumora," the owl repeated, "shall you not?"

Bess knew that she could not refuse. There were covenants, unwritten laws particular to each kind of owl. In general, these concerned acts of owl kindness that were to be performed selflessly. They were blessings not to be bestowed by Glaux but any ordinary owl. For a Boreal Owl to refuse to help one of its kind to die under a bell and sing them to glaumora was a profound violation of this unwritten code. So she helped the owl, dragging and pushing it as gently as possible, to the spot beneath the bell where her own father's bones had once rested. "What is your name?" She asked. But the sick owl had sunk into a delirium and was speaking gibberish. So now for the second time that evening, Bess rose and flew in the deep shadows of the bell's hood.

*I am the chimes in the night,*
*The sound within the wind.*
*I am the tolling of glaumora*
*For the souls of long-lost kin.*

*I shall sing you to the stars,*
*Where your scroom shall finally rest*
*'neath the great bell of the sky*
*In a tower of cloud crests.*

When she came to the last verse for this nameless owl, she felt none of her usual hope. It was hard to sing for an owl one did not know. But she sang on. He would be dead by morning, she was sure, but she would have done her duty. After finishing the ritual song she alighted near the Boreal's still form. The unknown owl roused himself and spoke in a low voice, "Go. Let me die alone, in peace."

Bess spent the night as she spent most of her nights, deep in study of ancient texts of the Others. Tonight her study was more solemn, shadowed by the thought of the dying owl. She had just begun her translation work for the fourth volume of the fragmentum, which was composed of scraps pieced together from the remains of some of the Others' great literary works. At the moment, she was working on some beautiful love sonnets attributed to the playwright known as Shakes. In between her scholarly labors, she took breaks to stretch her wings and fly the wonderful, swirling, misty gusts of the falls. As the night thinned, she went out to catch one of the plump water rats that scampered around the rocks at the falls' base. Then, before she turned in, she went to the bell tower to see if the owl had passed on.

He had not, but she was sure it would not be long. Bess could hear the owl's ragged breath from where she perched. She kept her distance as she watched, for once the final song had been sung it was customary to leave the owl so that there was no shadow other than the bell's cast upon it. The moon had long since slid into another world, but twixt time was nearing and the long shadows of morning would soon be upon the Palace of Mists.

She headed for the nest in the map hollow of the Palace of Mists where she now slept. It was not as comfortable as her previous sleeping place had been, a splendid hollow in the headless statue of an Other. Well, not quite an Other. It was a creature she had discovered through her research that the Others called an "angel," which was shaped like the Others — with the addition of huge wings. Whether or not angels truly ever existed, Bess could not determine. But the whole idea of the Others fashioning a likeness of themselves with wings struck Bess as rather poignant. She had found comfortable lodging in its right shoulder.

These days, however, she slept in the maparium. Bess almost dared not think about the reason for this change, as the secret was so vital to the well-being of the owl world that she feared merely thinking upon it could somehow put everything in danger.

In this chamber there were cabinets of ancient navigational instruments and strange artifacts. Its walls were honeycombed with deep, narrow cubbyholes. In those cubbyholes lay maps furled in metal tubes, a system which seemed to preserve them very well. The first time Bess tried sleeping in the maparium was during a spell of particularly awful weather. She had tried out more than a dozen sleeping places. First, the cubbyhole slots, which she hated; then she tried the case of a sextant, an instrument used by the Others for celestial navigation. But it was too shallow to get comfortable in. She had finally nested in a strange spherical map the Others had called a "globe." It had a rather large hole in it in the middle of an ocean labeled Pacific.

Upon entering the maparium, Bess, as she always did before settling into her new nesting place, perched for a moment in front of a collection in one of the largest cabinets. On the back wall of the cabinet, a map was mounted, and fixed to the map were a half dozen stone points, "arrowheads" the Others had called them. They seemed to be arranged on the map according to the regions the stones came from. The cabinet and its simple weapons suggested to Bess that the Others, now gone, had made a study of others preceding them. This thought inevitably brought on a gentle flurry of philosophical musings that usually lulled her to sleep. Bess felt her eyelids grow heavy.

She made her way to the globe and squeezed through

the hole in the Pacific Ocean. She settled in the pile of downy molted feathers and rabbit's ear moss with which she had made a reasonable lining. But sleep seemed to elude her. She bunched her feathers this way and that. Squashed back on her tail and stuck her legs straight out in front of her. Still sleep would not come. This was unusual for Bess. She wondered about the dying Boreal. How had he ever found his way to the Palace of Mists, sick as he was? It must have been purely by accident. Perhaps he had been flying over and was sucked into a downdraft. Too weak to fight, he just let himself go. That couldn't be quite right, because he had explicitly said that he wanted to die under a bell. So he must have known that this bell tower existed. Bess felt an uncomfortable squishiness in her gizzard. She wondered if he had died yet. Was his scroom climbing that star-chinked path to glaumora?

She finally fell into a fitful sleep. And as she slept, the tolling of the song she had sung echoed dimly somewhere in the back of her mind. It did not sound right. "I don't know why. I don't know why," she whispered in her sleep. She heard a familiar call. Her gizzard seemed to respond even as she slept. The call wound through her dream and she felt a flood of joy. "Da!" In all the long years she had been singing her father to glaumora, Bess had never once dreamed of him. But now he was floating in front of her in the silver dream-light that suffused her sleep! "Wake, silly child!" he exclaimed. With a jolt, she woke up. "It was a dream," she whispered to herself. But why in a dream should he call her to wake? *Something's wrong*, she thought. She pressed her eye against the crack in the globe to see if there just might be a scroom out there. Nothing. Nonetheless, she slipped out of the globe for a better look around the maparium.

And at that precise moment, Bess heard wing beats approaching. An acute sense of danger rattled her gizzard. It was too late to squeeze herself back into the globe. Desperately, she looked around for a hiding place. The door of the cabinet! She had left it open earlier and now flew directly toward it. Once inside, she wilfed and made herself as slender as the stone points, which were sharp. She would have to be careful.

The sun fell in a bright column from almost directly overhead, illuminating one of the busts of ancient explorers that lined the map hollow. The one they called Magellan. He wore a funny round hat and had a beard longer than any Whiskered Screech could hope for. Now a shadow fell across that beard, a short shadow due to the sun's angle, but recognizable nonetheless. Bess noted the slight dip in the crown of the head, the soft swoop of the brow tufts. It was a Boreal. And not just any Boreal, but the very one who had supposedly been poisoned and lay dying in the bell tower. Worse, it was wearing battle claws! Bess felt her gizzard tremble and then lock. She had been completely duped. And there was only one reason why an owl, a strange owl, would find his way to this place and attempt such a deception. The ember!

## CHAPTER FOUR

# *Scholar or Warrior?*

Bess was a scholar. She had never fought. Never worn battle claws, never held a weapon, never even wielded a burning branch — perish the thought! There must be no flames in the Palace of Mists with its treasure trove of books and maps. But now she knew that Bess the scholar would have to change. Was she up to it? Did she have a choice? She had no doubt that the intruder was after the ember. How many places in the palace had the Boreal Owl searched so far? If he went through the passageway and was persistent enough, he would find the spiraling tunnel to the stone chamber, the one the Others had called the "crypt." It was a burial vault that contained coffins and the relics of great scholars. It was in one of these coffins that Bess had placed the cask that held the Ember of Hoole.

The Ember of Hoole presented baffling and often dangerous choices to those entrusted with its keeping. Forged in the fires of the Sacred Ring of volcanoes in a time before time, retrieved more than a thousand years ago by Hoole, it was this peculiar and powerful ember that anointed the true kings of Ga'Hoole. There would be other monarchs, good ones, but to be an embered monarch was very special. There had only been two in the entire thousand-year history of the tree: Hoole and Coryn.

With the ember came many blessings. But it seemed that with every blessing there came a curse. For the ember contained in its fiery gizzard a power for both good and bad — for bad especially in the talons of a weak or evil owl. One had to be exceedingly careful in its presence. Hoole, an owl of exceptional mettle, withstood these influences. However, it had been so long since owls had lived under the rule of an embered king that they were not always prepared for the dangers it posed.

Now wedged between two lethal-looking stone arrowheads, Bess thought of the tribulations that had accompanied the ember since Coryn had retrieved it. Many of the owls of the great tree had fallen under the ember's thrall and had begun to worship it; then sometime later the Striga, the strange blue owl from the Middle Kingdom, came to exert a malignant influence over Coryn and to seek even greater power by seizing the ember. *Thank Glaux,* Bess thought, *he had failed.*

Would Bess fail to protect the ember now? Would she fail to act? The minutes lengthened; the shadows, too, as the sun passed its zenith. The silhouette of the Boreal Owl began to slide over the cabinet. Would he turn toward the passageway that led to the crypt? Should she wait? She did not complete the thought but seized two sharp stone points, one in each talon, burst from the cabinet, and flew at the Boreal Owl.

She flew directly for the owl's gizzard and would have landed a fatal blow except for the glancing swipe of one of the intruder's battle-clawed talons which sent her reeling. Blood spun through the air. At first, Bess was not sure where it came from, but then realized the blood was not her own. She saw it stream from the underside of the intruder's wing, a spot called the wing-pit. Had she struck the gizzard or the heart it would have meant his instant death. The owl staggered in his flight, and Bess was relieved to see his wounded wing droop. Confusion swam in the owl's eyes. But Bess's relief did not last for long. The furious owl hurtled wildly toward her with startling speed despite his wound. The arrowhead fell to the floor with a clink. The intruder attempted to seize it, but missed and, in one swift, graceful movement, Bess shoved it out of his way with a sweep of her wing tip, and then quickly retrieved it for herself. The two owls now began circling each other. Bess knew nothing about the strategies of talon-to-talon combat, or of fighting defensively. Her gizzard pulsed wildly. She was definitely out of her element. And she could tell that this Boreal Owl was a seasoned combat soldier.

"Where is it?" the owl demanded.

"Where is what?" she parried.

"The Ember of Hoole."

"I know nothing of any ember."

"You don't expect me to believe that!"

Still they circled. It was as if Bess's brain was operating on two levels. On one, she was trying to fight, on the other, she was trying to parry with words, upset this owl's equilibrium as she had done with the jab to the wingpit, but mentally, gizzardly.

"I never expected a Boreal Owl to abuse the tolling ritual. What you did was a profanity." Did she detect a slight flinching of plumage, as if the owl was about to wilf? "Forget glaumora," she added. "You'll rot in hagsmire."

"Never!" the owl spat vehemently. "We shall control hagsmire and all its fiends."

Now it was Bess who flinched. What was this owl talking about? The Boreal Owl saw his opening in the fraction of time Bess had let her mind wander. The owl rushed in and struck her to the stone floor. The wind was knocked from her and she heard the clink once more of a stone point as it fell to the floor. She still held one in her talon. She saw a flash as the Boreal Owl flew for the spiraling stairs. *The crypt!* She banished all thoughts from her brain and in that utterly mindless moment, Bess of the Chimes, Bess the Knower, became a warrior. She would not think. She would not feel. She would only kill. She blasted through the air like a missile. Down, down, down into the crypt, she spiraled on the tail of the other Boreal. They zigzagged through the maze of stone. Bess heard the clank of the battle claws as the owl skimmed a corner. This owl was not a precision flier. *I am better at this,* Bess thought. He couldn't even pick up the arrowhead when he had knocked it from her talons. *A clear shot, that's all I need. One clear shot.* Bess began to drive the owl out from the narrow alleys between the stone coffins. There was a bay at the back of the crypt. If she could get him to fly there, he would be trapped. She must make him think the ember was in that bay. That was it! She stopped her flight and reversed her direction suddenly, and began to carve a turn toward the bay. The owl took the bait. He thought she was flying back to defend the ember.

And now an odd thing transpired. Bess felt as if she were actually becoming two owls. There was Bess the warrior, the strategist who swiveled her head back and tried to muster a fearsome look in her eyes, and then there was Bess the observer. The Bess she knew. Bess now pretended to dart from her course, but gave her opponent ample berth to block the move. *It's working! It's working!* They were almost in the bay. There were a few niches in the walls where candles had once burned to light the crypt. She flew directly toward one, then did an inside-out loop and hovered against the niche with her wings spread wide as if she were protecting something — something precious.

"Let me at it or I'll tear you to pieces," the intruder screeched.

Bess said nothing. She continued to hover against the stone wall. Now she did not have to feign fear. She *was* frightened. Her gizzard twitched in spasms of pure terror. But she must hold steady and draw him closer. She heard the click of the battle claws as he extended them.

The serrated edges gleamed and then blurred as the Boreal charged. Bess bunched her shoulder and raised her talon, and the air glinted as bits of mica embedded in the arrowhead flashed like shooting stars.

And then it was over.

Bess blinked. Beneath her, the Boreal Owl had fallen. From its breast, an arrowhead protruded. And now the owl was truly gasping its last breath on earth. Bess bent over the dying owl.

"I suppose now you expect me to toll you to glaumora."

The amber eyes growing tarnished as life seeped from him suddenly brightened with a horrifying glint. "I am in hag's cradle now. Hagsmire is my glaumora. You will see. Just wait . . . just . . ." But the words evaporated as the owl met death.

"Death profane," Bess whispered. She was no longer Bess the warrior. She had stepped back inside her own body and only now realized that she was shaking uncontrollably.

CHAPTER FIVE

# A Wolf and a Bear

Sveep trundled along the overland route. She had never been out of the Northern Kingdoms before. And perhaps it was insane not to be swimming. But the katabats had begun to blow earlier, as Svarr had predicted, and the pack ice was being driven down faster than she had anticipated. She was not sure that the puffin would get up his nerve to go to the owls. She had told him to go, but would he? She felt she had to do something despite the weariness, the lethargy that afflicted all polar bears with the coming of winter. A backup plan was needed. The backup plan was the she-wolf, Gyllbane, her old friend. She would go to her and tell her what the puffin had seen.

There was one thing of which she was certain. She was not carrying babies this season. It was nice to have a rest. Beneath the call of winter's long sleep, she felt a new energy. And who would want to bring young cubs into such a world, anyway, if what she could piece together from the puffin's jumbled narrative was true?

She had made Gyllbane's acquaintance perhaps three summers ago. The wolf was racked with grief over the loss of her son and, as she said, needed to get away. Sveep had just given birth to her second set of cubs, and Gyllbane proved herself remarkably helpful with them. Auntie Gyll, the cubs had begun to call her almost as soon as they could speak. Sveep knew that Gyllbane had been very close to Coryn, the monarch of the Great Ga'Hoole Tree. She had shared so much with Gyllbane, and Gyllbane with her. And she knew she must share this, too.

Sveep had been traveling two days and was now approaching Broken Talon Point. The landscape had begun to change contrasting sharply with the treeless world from which Sveep had come. There was not a trace of snow, and what had been a sprinkling of trees soon thickened into groves of tall firs and spruce. Sveep had little use for trees but she could appreciate the quiet grandeur with which they rose from this otherwise barren landscape. She knew that farther into the Beyond, the trees became fewer again. As Gyllbane had explained, it was a harsh, stark landscape.

It was not far from here that she knew Gyllbane made her summer camp. She would be closing in on it soon. She had to remember not to call the wolf by her old name. She was no longer Gyllbane, but Namara. Since Sveep had last seen her, the wolf had become the chieftain of the MacNamaras — a clan distinguished by both extreme intelligence and toughness.

In the country known as the Beyond, each wolf clan had its own territory, but the MacNamara territory was at some remove from the rest. They joined the other clans on the seasonal byrrgis, the formations for hunting, and came for the various all-clan gatherings at the Sacred Ring. But the MacNamara clan preferred to keep its distance from the others.

Suddenly, from behind a fir tree, a small wolf pup scampered out. The pup could not have been more than six moons old. It looked plump, and Sveep realized for the first time that she was hungry. Of course, it wouldn't do to eat a wolf pup. But she wondered now what she would do for food. She was far from the sea. The salt tang had faded and with it her customary food choices — fish, the occasional seal, otter. All the delicious choices of the Northern Kingdoms. What in the name of Ursa did one eat around here? Trees? She plodded on, hoping the pup would keep its distance. She didn't want to deal with the temptation. It was a curious little critter, all fluff, and yapping now.

"Are you real? I mean really real?" the pup asked Sveep.

Sveep kept going and tried not to look at the pup. "Of course I'm real. Aren't you?"

"Oh, yes. You bet. Almost six moons old. Another moon and I get to go on my first byrrgis. You're a polar bear, aren't you?"

"Indeed." Sveep said as little as possible.

"You're bigger than a grizzly. We'd have a hard time taking you down to eat. I think we'd need two clans to do it. So don't worry."

*Me, worry?* Sveep thought.

"Crannog!" A beautiful silver she-wolf exploded from some brush. It ran straight toward Sveep then immediately lowered her body. Pressing her belly to the ground, she flattened her ears and flashed the whites of her eyes. "Show some manners, Crannog," she growled to her pup. The little pup immediately crouched down.

Sveep stopped short. She had heard that the dire wolves of the Beyond had strange ways, but this beat all. They were scraping on their bellies toward Sveep. What in the name of Ursa was going on? "We have heard of your kind from Namara," the she-wolf said.

"Yes, yes, I am an old friend of Gyll . . . Namara. I have important news for her. I must see her right away. Point me in the right direction."

The she-wolf stopped groveling. "Point you in right direction!" she almost shrieked. "You think ye can just barge into her den?" The wolf had an odd accent, a sing-songy voice that Sveep now remembered was similar to that of Gyllbane.

"Well . . . well, let her know I'm here. But I've got to see her immediately."

The wolf now drew herself up to her full height. The sun was setting, washing the land with a soft pink-orange light. Her silvery fur seemed to shimmer. "My name is Blair. How do ye call yourself?"

"Sveep."

"Ah!" she replied. She nodded her head slightly.

"You know me?"

"I know of ye. I know that you are the bear that Namara, when she was still Gyllbane, shared a cave with somewhere far north of here. It was the time when she be sick with grief for her son, Cody. I know you were a great comfort to her and that she done poured out her grief until she was left so weak she could not eat and that you fed her some of the milk from your own teats. Milk that was for your cubs."

"Oh, my cubs were fat. I had milk to spare."

"She might have died had you not." She sighed. "But she did not tell you of our peculiar ways, I suppose. You saw what I did —" She paused. "— And what my son did not do — when I first came up to you?"

"Yes."

"I made the gestures a wolf would make to one of higher rank." She then turned to her pup, who was still groveling on the ground. "And until this young'un learns, he shall not go on any byrrgis." A little whine came from the pile of fur. The pup had hidden his eyes behind his paws in shame. Only the pink of his nose could be seen. Blair continued in her lilting voice. "We have our codes of conduct. The Gaddernock we call it; the way of the dire wolf clans. Now follow me and I will take you to the Gadderheal, our ceremonial cave."

"But I just want to see Gyll . . . I mean, Namara, in her own den. This need not be so . . . so formal."

"Oh, it's not a matter of formality."

"What is it, then?"

"It's the only place you'll fit."

CHAPTER SIX

# Namara Howls

"You say the puffin said something about hagsfiends." Namara's eyes glistened like resplendent twin emeralds in the dark gloom of the cave. Outside, tree limbs creaked in a sudden wind. Sveep nodded. "And then you say the other owl, the blue one, said something about the Ember of Hoole?"

"Not exactly in that order," Sveep replied. "First, the blue owl said that he knew all about the ember. And then the other owl said something about hagsfiends."

Namara's eyes became green slits. Her hackles rose stiffly, and her ears stood up straight. She began padding about the cave in a tight circle. "This is bad . . . very bad."

"I know nothing about the ember or hagsfiends," Sveep said. "This is all owl business, isn't it?"

"Yes . . ." Then Namara stopped and peered at her old friend, who had been so helpful to her in the time of her overwhelming grief. "But it is our business, as well.

All of us." She paused again. "Cody." Her voice broke as she spoke her son's name, remembering that last image of him dead atop the *Book of Kreeth,* his throat slashed. "Cody died trying to save the world from hagsfiends."

"But I thought they were just creatures of legends, very old legends, and as the owl said, have been gone for a thousand years." There was a desperate note in Sveep's voice as if she were grasping for some small thread of hope.

"I thought that, too, but Coryn told me that the legends, are not mere legends. This book, the one they called the *Book of Kreeth,* was an ancient tome that had belonged to an arch hagsfiend. It was thought to have formulas and designs for all sorts of haggish inventions and creations. That is why the Guardians fought so hard in the Beyond, to keep it from Nyra and the Pure Ones, and why we helped them."

Sveep knew that Gyllbane and Coryn were about as close as a wolf and an owl could be. It was Gyllbane who had been there when Coryn had retrieved the Ember of Hoole. "And tell me, Sveep," the wolf continued, "the other owl — what did the puffin say it looked like?"

"Terrible. The puffin said he wasn't sure if it was a Great Horned, a Barn Owl, or what. He thought maybe a Barn Owl, but its feathers were dark and raggedy at the ends. Almost black like a crow's and when it turned its face, it was terribly scarred."

Namara lowered her head and shook it back and forth mournfully. "How has this happened? Cody can't have died in vain. It can't be true." But she knew it was. Somehow an evil had started to seep back into their peaceful universe. *What was the word owls used? Nachtmagen? Yes, nachtmagen was . . .* The wolf could not finish the thought. She trotted out of the Gadderheal. A full moon blazed in the sky. She stood in a silver column of its light and, throwing her head back, began to howl the strange mad music of wolves. These were not the cries of mourning. Of this much even Sveep could tell. Savage and untamed, this was a howl of rage.

Namara's wolves stirred in their dens, and the wind carried her howls to those more distant clans. No other creatures knew the meaning of the wolves' howling. They only knew that once it started, it did not end for hours. The grizzly bear, the moose, the caribou, the jackrabbits, the birds that flew overhead, felt the song drill into every part of their beings. But what did it mean, this wild song? For that is what the other creatures of the Beyond called it. They would whisper to one another in their dens or burrows, "They are wild singing again." "It's the moon," one would say. Then another would argue,

"No, it's not the moon. It can be moonless and still they sing." "They're crazy!" another might say.

But the wolves were anything but crazy. They were among the most organized and methodical of animals in everything they did, from how they hunted to their strategies for traveling to the rearing of their young. Their howling was as systematic as any language, and through it they could convey an enormous range of information. Now on this night hundreds of wolves began to leave their dens and form byrrgises. So the call had gone out to break summer camp and meet in the Gadderheal of the Sacred Ring of volcanoes. The owl kingdoms were imperiled and so was the world of every living creature.

In a rocky redoubt near the volcanoes of the Sacred Ring there was a masked owl, a Rogue smith by the name of Gwyndor. He looked up from his forge, where he had just put to use the excellent bonk coals he had acquired from one of the colliers. Namara's first howls were too far from the volcanoes for any creature near them to hear at first but as the byrrgises made their way toward the Sacred Ring, the howling continued and the approach of the wolves was known.

Gwyndor had spent more years than any other owl

in the Beyond. And he had become a student of wolves. Although he did not know even the very general meaning of the howls, he could recognize the voices of many of the clan chiefs. The wolf who led the howling varied, depending on the situation, and that wolf was called the skreeleen. This time the skreeleen was Namara. He was sure of it. And if it was Namara, Gwyndor knew it was not an ordinary situation. Not a herd of caribou migrating through the MacNamara territory, or a wolf sick with the foaming-mouth disease, or a grizzly fishing in the river. She would let another high-ranking wolf of her clan convey that type of information. But when Namara howled, which was rare, it was about owls. And although Gwyndor did not know the meaning, he detected a vibration in the timbre of her cries that hearkened back to that dreadful night when owl and wolf fought flank to wing and her only pup had been killed. He felt a dread build in his gizzard. The byrrgises of the clans that were converging on the Sacred Ring were still several hours away. It would be daybreak when they arrived. Should he wait or fly out to meet Namara, get her awful news, and then fly on to the great tree to deliver it? He had been a slipgizzle for the great tree for some time now. The Sacred Ring was a good place to pick up information, because so many

Rogue colliers came to dive the coal beds from all parts of the Southern Kingdoms. But if he waited, he would be forced to fly in daylight, and crow mobbings had been on the rise lately. And how much would he learn if he waited? One really couldn't interrupt a byrrgis, nor would he be permitted into a Gadderheal. But Coryn would. Coryn had a special relationship with the wolves. With Namara in particular.

He decided that he must leave immediately for the great tree. The wind had shifted. He should be able to make it at least as far as the border between the Shadow Forest and Silverveil. Of course, if he flew over the spirit woods it would be even shorter and safer. Crows never entered the spirit woods, but he felt himself wilf at the thought. Gwyndor had never encountered a scroom and although it was said they were perfectly harmless he was not anxious to meet up with any, either.

Another owl far from the Beyond was perched on the very top of the bell tower trying to decide not *when* she should leave for the Great Ga'Hoole Tree, but *if* she *could* leave. Bess had not left the Palace of Mists since she had first arrived years before. The farthest she had ever flown since that time was to the base of the water-falls to hunt. The mist-shrouded cleft in the Shadow

Forest provided everything she needed. And the Boreal Owl, as she had grown older, hoarded her solitude like a miser hoarding gold. It was priceless. She had sworn years before after the arduous journey in which she had transported her father's bones that she would never leave this palace. It was her paradise, her own glaumora on earth. She found all the company she required in books and ideas. Over the years, her long-distance flight skills had become as rusty as the hinges on the palace doors. She knew all one could about navigation, for she had read all the books of the old explorers, but could she do it on the wing? Now, as she perched on the edge of the bell tower, she wondered if she had the courage to leave this place. Her gizzard rebelled at the very thought. Who would toll for her father?

She was happy that her father had not come to her as a scroom, for that would mean he had unfinished business on earth. Instead her father had appeared in a dream and said, "Wake!" Maybe that meant she should leave her concerns of scholarship and theory and go out into the world. The facts were pretty straightforward. An owl lay dead in the palace. She had killed that owl. He lay in a pool of blood, an arrowhead buried in his breast. And now she must go out into the world. She must fly to the great tree and tell the shocking news of the intruder who spoke of hags and hagsmire and demanded the ember. And if one owl knew the ember was at the Palace of Mists, did others?

Bess shut her eyes. *I can't go! I can't! I am so scared.* She felt her gizzard clench. A warm draft of air rose up from below. Such warm drafts or thermals were rare. Was it a sign? These thermals were the easiest to fly, giving owls a sturdy boost, allowing them to soar with hardly a wing waggle for propulsion. It seemed as if the very elements were conspiring against her fear. *Or are they conspiring* for *me? Trying to entice me into the sky?*

She felt pressed now between this rising thermal and that pool of blood in the crypt. She closed her eyes, gave a sudden small yelp, and flung herself onto the warm breast of the updraft. *Here goes nothing!* she thought. And felt the warm air fold around her like the wings of her da.

## CHAPTER SEVEN

# *I'm Here!*

The days had shortened and the nights had grown longer. In the few daylight hours left, the owls slept deeply, recovering from all the work and play of the season of long nights. Since her injury of the previous year, Otulissa found that she had to rebuild her strength gradually and often retired earlier than the other owls, taking a few hours of quiet reflection before sleep. There had been a string of sparkling days in the season of the Copper-Rose Rain, and since she had not exhausted herself flying all night long she often retreated to her favorite spot in the Great Ga'Hoole Tree — the hanging garden. It was her chosen place for reflection. The pockets of the tree, where the major limbs joined the trunk, had always collected a variety of organic matter. It had been customary to clear this out several times a year as it was thought to be better for the health of the tree. Otulissa had supervised this chore. But in Otulissa's capacity of Ga'Hoolology ryb, she had begun a series of experiments in which she let the organic matter accumulate. She discovered that with careful management of the small shrubs, lichens, and plants that took root in the pockets, the overall health of the tree was enhanced. Indeed, many of the plants in the hanging gardens offered additional crops that could be gathered for food. A new variety of nooties, similar to the ones that could be harvested during the time of the Copper-Rose Rain, now grew during other seasons. Aside from the nutritional benefits of the cultivated pockets, there was the sheer beauty of their hanging gardens; the mosses, lichens, and many flowering plants — including orchids — were suspended like colorful constellations from the canopy of the tree.

On this morning, with the sun bouncing off the rosy golden milkberries, the tree seemed spangled with light. Cleve joined her, as did Tengshu, her old friend from the sixth kingdom, who was staying for a spell in the tree. So successful had the Greenowls — trained by Tengshu — been in routing the Striga and his troops from the great tree, that Coryn had decided upon the formation of a new chaw so that Guardians could learn Danyar, the fighting discipline practiced by the blue owls of the Middle Kingdom. Tengshu was here to teach to them.

"I do feel, Cleve dear, that perhaps we owls, being night creatures, have underrated the splendor of the day."

"Perhaps. But it is hard to imagine flying about in the daylight with a scalding sun blasting your wings. Daylight has no texture. It's not like the night. There are no stars, none of the black feathery softness of the evening."

"Oh, Cleve, just listen to your prejudice. You define everything in owl terms — saying the black is feathery."

"I agree," Tengshu said. "You know, in the Middle Kingdom, we do quite a bit of day flying, since we have no crows, and need not fear mobbing. I was flying about just now. There is a new freshness in the air." He hesitated. "I don't know how to describe it. Should I say 'thump of wind' coming in from the north?"

"Ah, the katabats!" Cleve said.

"The katabats?" Tengshu asked.

"Yes, that's what we call them in the Northern Kingdoms where they originate. You're just feeling the very outermost fringes of them," Otulissa said, then continued. "They are actually caused by a reverse cyclonic inversion . . ."

"Your knowledge, madam, astounds me," Tengshu exclaimed quickly. Then he paused a moment. "I think

I've seen that Short-eared Owl with the russet feathers, sensational flier, taking a daytime flight."

"Ruby, of course," Otulissa and Cleve both said at once.

"Yes, Ruby."

"Ruby flies night or day." Otulissa laughed. "If there's a good wind to be caught she is out there." And then rather slyly, Otulissa swiveled her head in Cleve's direction. "Do ask Ruby, my dear, about the texture of the day as compared to the night."

"Ha!" Cleve churred heartily.

Just at that moment they heard something flapping loudly above them. They all flipped their heads straight up to see what it was.

"Great Glaux, what is that thing?" Tengshu exclaimed.

"I'm coming in! I'm coming in! Mind your heads," the thing called out. "I'm not so good at this!"

A flash of orange sliced through a cascade of orchids that swung from the upper level of the hanging garden. "Oh, Great Glaux! There goes my *Cymbidium strumella*!" Otulissa shrieked as the lovely yellow-speckled blossoms of the orchid swirled around them.

There was a soft plop as Dumpy belly flopped on a hummock of moss. "Am I here? Am I actually here?"

he gasped, looking up into the faces peering down at him.

"That depends. What was your intended destination?" Otulissa asked.

"Destination?" Dumpy repeated.

"Oh, Glaux," Otulissa murmured. She'd forgotten how dumb puffins were. Why was this one here? They rarely left the Ice Narrows. "Where did you want to go?" She spoke slowly and distinctly as one might to a very young child.

"Uh . . . the great tree. The great tree. Big news. Big, big news!"

"Well, then you have arrived at your destination," Cleve said.

"And what is the big news?" Otulissa asked.

Dumpy staggered to his feet. "Uh . . . I was afraid you were going to ask me that."

"Why were you afraid?" Tengshu tipped his head forward.

Dumpy stared so hard at Tengshu his eyes nearly popped out of his head. "Oh, Great Ice! Another one!"

"Another what?" the three owls asked at once.

"He looks just like the other blue owl I saw." Dumpy nodded at Tengshu. "Except this one's prettier. More feathers."

Otulissa gasped. "It can't be!" she whispered.

Cleve took a step forward and put a protective wing around Dumpy's plump shoulders. "Now, son."

"I'm not your son," Dumpy said with sudden alarm. "I'm not nearly smart enough to be an owl. And I can tell you that if I were your son, I'd be a great disappointment to you."

"It's just an expression," Otulissa interjected.

Dumpy suddenly looked up at Cleve. "Oh, Good Ice, I know . . . who you are." Dumpy began to sputter. "You're the owl who took the sea tick from my foot." He lifted up one of his webbed feet and began waving it about until he fell over. "Good as new!" he said as he picked himself up and flopped against Cleve's chest, embracing him.

"Let's get to the bottom of this," Otulissa continued.

"Oh, yes, I have a bottom!" Dumpy said, and immediately turned around and tipped his butt into the air.

Otulissa leaned toward Tengshu and whispered, "You must understand that puffins can be very literal. So we must just stick to the basics. Now, Dumpy, you did say your name was Dumpy, didn't you?"

"Yes," Dumpy said with some uncertainty.

"Concentrate, dear," Otulissa went on. "You say you saw a blue owl."

Dumpy shut his eyes very tightly and appeared to be concentrating with every bit of brain he possessed. He began to speak very slowly.

"You see, there is this ice cave and I know a back way in, and I saw these two owls go in there, so I sneaked in the back way and listened . . ."

"Two owls, not just one?"

"Yes, two. But only one was blue. Blue? I just learned the name for that color. I used to call it 'sky,' but from the polar bear I learned it's blue."

"Polar bear — how does a polar bear fit into this?" Cleve asked.

"Oh, the polar bear didn't fit into the ice cave. No, I had to fly to the polar bear and tell her about what they said because I didn't know half their words, words like 'hagsfiend.'"

"HAGSFIEND!" the three owls gasped.

Meanwhile, on the far side of the great tree, unbeknownst to Otulissa, Cleve, and Tengshu, another unlikely visitor had arrived and gone directly to Soren.

## CHAPTER EIGHT

# Astonishing Visitors

Yoicks!" blurted Twilight. "It's absolutely yoicks." The Great Gray had taken the words out of all their beaks. Soren swiveled his head, first one way and then the other. He blinked at this motley crew: Dumpy the puffin, Gwyndor, and the most astonishing visitor of all — Bess — Bess who had never in their experience dared leave the Palace of Mists.

*Yoicks, indeed,* thought Soren. Bess had arrived on the branch outside his hollow as he and Pelli and their children were about to take tea. Completely exhausted, feathers askew from the tumultuous flight, she was an alarming sight. The three B's stared at her wide-eyed. Pelli was speechless. Gulping to catch her breath, Bess said, "I came right here. Soren, I must see the king and the rest of the Band." He had tried to get her to rest, take a spot of milkberry tea. But she had shouted, which in itself was shocking, for Bess always spoke in a low melodious voice, "There is no time for tea!"

So they had gone to Coryn's hollow, only to find the puffin, Dumpy, already there with Otulissa, Tengshu, and Cleve.

"All right," said Coryn, "let's start again at the beginning so Soren and the Band can hear. Take this from the top, as the expression goes."

Dumpy immediately tried to stand on his head.

"That won't be necessary, dear," Gylfie said, and flashed a look at Otulissa as if to say, *How will we ever get through this?*

Little by little the story came out. A fragment here, a sliver there. Threads, snippets. No one individual had the whole piece but when these shreds were pieced together there emerged a grim design indeed — on a diabolical cloth.

"Now, let's review what we know," Coryn said. "The ember. You are sure, Bess, that is what the Boreal Owl was after? He actually said the word?"

"He said 'Where is it?' and I said, 'Where is what?' And he said. 'The Ember of Hoole.' And I said. 'I know nothing of any ember.'"

"And then you killed him."

"Well, it wasn't quite that quick. We fought. But, yes. I killed him. He's dead." All the owls looked at one another and shook their heads in wonder. Bess, the timid scholar, had killed an owl!

"So we must assume that this Boreal Owl is not the only one who knows about the ember," Soren spoke softly.

"I didn't know what to think," Bess replied. "I was torn about what to do. Whether to fly here with the ember. But if there were other owls who knew I might be carrying it, I could be ambushed. It seemed best to leave it hidden where it is."

"I think that was the best decision," Coryn said. "But now, turning toward this other matter." There was a sharp, quick stab like a pinprick in all of their gizzards. By "other matter" they knew Coryn meant hagsfiends.

"Kreeth's book is still here," Otulissa said. "It was the first thing I checked on after we ousted the Striga, or rather the first thing Fritha checked, since I was so badly wounded. There is no way he could have studied that book. It's been under lock and key since the time we took it. . . ." She hesitated, for the searing image was still sharp in her mind, as it was in the minds of the other owls who had been there: Cody's bloodied and broken body crumpled atop the book. Indeed, the book still bore stains of the young wolf's blood. She turned toward Dumpy.

"Dumpy, now concentrate," Otulissa said. This was about the fifth time the owls had asked him to concentrate and he was beginning to find it easier. "Can your recall exactly what you heard about hagsfiends?"

Dumpy closed his eyes again and clamped his beak shut for a moment, then spoke. "I think I can. The blue owl said hagsfiends vanished nearly one thousand years ago. Then the dark owl said, 'So you think they are gone forever?' The blue owl said, 'Madame General, what are you suggesting?' and the dark owl said, 'I am suggesting nothing is forever.' And the blue owl said he wasn't good at riddles. And then the dark owl said something about the Long Night. 'A marvelous hatching will occur.' The blue owl asked, 'There is an egg?' And the dark owl said, 'Soon.'"

Dumpy paused and looked at his audience of owls. "Hey, what happened to you guys? You all got so skinny," Dumpy said.

In the space of Dumpy's very admirable recitation all the owls had wilfed to half their normal size.

Soren regained his composure first. "Dumpy, that was an excellent job you did just now. I have one question."

"Yes?"

"Why do you keep calling the one owl the 'dark owl'?"

"Well, at first I thought the owl was a Barn Owl, the shape of her face, you know, and the length of her wings, and her height. And I thought I saw some of those speckles like you have on your shoulders. But her feathers weren't that pretty golden color like yours."

Otulissa blinked. This was a rather detailed description for a puffin to be rendering. In fact, all the owls in the hollow were astonished that a puffin could hold so many logically connected thoughts in its mind. "But," Dumpy continued, "her feathers were so dark, almost black. And they were long and shaggy. At least the edges were. She almost looked like a crow, but uglier."

*Hagsfiend!* The word hung unspoken and dreadful in the dim light of the hollow like a curse rising from hagsmire. And each owl felt a terrible clench deep in its gizzard.

Gylfie was the first to speak. "And the face. You say it was the shape of a Barn Owl's"

Dumpy nodded.

"But what else about it? Were her feathers white like Soren's and her eyes black?"

"Her face was scarred. Especially on one side. I didn't

see it at first until she took off the mask and hung it on an ice pick. But then it was awful. I'd never seen such an awful face. One scar . . ." Dumpy hesitated and stole a glance at Coryn. "One scar cut across her face like yours — begging your pardon, your face is much more handsome — and her eyes, well, they weren't completely black like yours. Something flickered deep inside them — a pale yellow light."

Coryn's anguish was palpable. He sighed deeply. "So we now know for certain that Nyra lives. Indeed, she wears a mask like that of my father, Kludd, made presumably from its scraps. And she grows haggish."

"Where she found a Rogue smith to fix that mask for her, I'll never know!" Gwyndor seethed.

"Any kind of creature can be bought. Owls ain't no different," Bubo said.

This news was shocking. But Coryn seemed to recover and to expand. His plumage puffed until he was enormous. "The Striga and Nyra are in collusion. Now we know. We shall act. We shall not let ourselves be terrorized or intimidated. We have the advantage of knowing that they are up to something." Coryn's eyes were blazing. Soren felt his gizzard stir with pride. He had not seen Coryn so strong, so steady, so resolute in a long time. The young king had spent a large part of his life haunted by the violent history of his parents, Kludd and Nyra. Raised by the most ruthless mother owl imaginable, he was no stranger to tyranny. He now turned to the puffin, Gwyndor, and Bess, who stood side by side, and began to speak. "You three birds have shown extraordinary courage and wit."

Dumpy blinked.

*Wit! He's saying I have wit!*

"Each of you was alert and ready to act. Gwyndor, with your keen ear for the wolves, you were able to discern the voice of my dear friend Gyllbane and realized that even though you were not sure of the exact meaning of the howls, that she was deeply agitated. You knew that she was skreeling as she had when she led the byrrgis for the battle of the *Book of Kreeth.*

"And you, dear Bess, defended the ember with a courage the equal of any in battle. You left your cherished refuge and flew for the first time into the night world of owls and crossed the Sea of Hoolemere. We know how difficult this must have been."

Coryn took a step closer to the puffin. "And you, Dumpy, the debt we owe you is incalculable. You observed carefully, remembered all, and first flew to the polar bear. It was she who said 'This is owl business' and that you must go to the Great Ga'Hoole Tree. And you did! You found us and you related what you saw and what you heard with great intelligence."

Dumpy blinked rapidly. "I think I'm going to faint." His squat, usually well-balanced body suddenly wobbled. Bubo stepped in and propped him up.

"Here you go, lad. Now steady there."

When Dumpy had regained his balance, Coryn continued. "It seems we have a situation developing here. There are two issues. First, the ember. Someone is hunting for it. Obviously someone knows it is no longer here at the great tree. How many owls know? Was this Boreal an agent for others? We cannot be sure. Bess?"

"It is possible, Coryn, that this owl was working alone. If there were others, why would they not have come to help? He duped me, yes, with the ruse of being poisoned. Had he come with cohorts, they could have easily infiltrated the palace while I . . . I . . ." She hesitated. "Tolled him to glaumora."

"And instead, you sent him to hagsmire!" Twilight boomed. "I like it! I like it a lot! A most artistic balance. Like a good story. All set to rights in the end."

Gylfie gave the Great Gray a withering look.

"Well," Coryn said, "his part of the story has ended but we must try to set the rest to rights. Which brings me to the second issue. It appears that Nyra herself is . . . is . . ." For the first time, Coryn faltered, then regained his confidence. "Is becoming more haggish. How this is happening, what peculiar physiological changes are occurring . . ." He swiveled his head toward Otulissa as if seeking some clue, some thread of an explanation.

"It's very strange," Otulissa said. "We have all read about hagsfiends in the past. The *Book of Kreeth* is mostly a speculative work on how one might create monstrous haggish offspring through various experiments. But what Dumpy describes suggests a morphological reversion to a more primitive form. We know from the battle in the canyonlands that in certain phases of the moon, given the right conditions and the ingestion of contaminated water, wolves, corrupt ones such as those of the MacHeath clan, could become vyrwolves, while other wolves were completely immune to such changes. Perhaps we have a similar situation here."

Soren swiveled his head toward Otulissa. "These thoughts of yours are interesting, Otulissa, but we must plan. Now is not the time for speculation."

"You are right, Soren." Otulissa nodded in agreement.

"I think," Soren said, swiveling his head toward his nephew, Coryn, "we need a plan to secure the ember. We can hope that the Boreal Owl Bess killed was the only one who knew about it. If this is the case we must assume that he planned to steal it for his own purposes."

"What purposes?" asked Digger.

"Well, perhaps he wanted to ransom it or sell it to the highest bidder. Perhaps he was planning to approach Nyra."

"In any case," Otulissa said, "the ember must be removed as soon as possible from the Palace of Mists. We have to assume that the palace is now vulnerable. It is just too risky to suppose that the Boreal was working alone."

Bess sighed. "I am so glad you said that, Otulissa. The owl had battle claws. I killed him with the stone points. But I shudder to think what might have happened if that owl had brought fire into the palace." A silence fell upon the group. The Palace of Mists possessed a treasury of books, maps, documents, and artifacts that had in the last few years advanced the culture and technologies of owls in ways they could never have imagined.

"But if we send someone to retrieve the ember," Bubo said, "that owl could be followed."

"That's true," Soren said slowly. He blinked his eyes shut for several seconds. Gylfie, Soren's oldest friend, looked at him. After years of diving into forest fires his beak had lost its tawny glow and was permanently smudged. But he still had that dark sparkle in his eyes, and his face feathers had retained their luster. The two owls knew each other so well that words were not always necessary. Right now, Gylfie sensed what Soren was thinking. "Gylfie," Soren turned to the Elf Owl. "Do your remember back at St. Aggie's when we discovered that Hortense was actually an infiltrator, and how she told us she had arrived there?"

"Of course!" Gylfie's yellow eyes blazed. She knew exactly where Soren was heading with this. "HALO!" she exclaimed.

## CHAPTER NINE

# Tactics

"HALO?" Gwyndor asked.

"High Altitude Low Opening situation," Otulissa replied. "Of course!"

"What?" Bubo asked.

"Huh?" Dumpy said. "What's altitude?"

Coryn shot Otulissa a warning glance as she sighed and muttered something about Dumpy's limited vocabulary. Gylfie began to explain. "It's a stealth strategy for getting into an area without being noticed. You wait for a night with thick cloud cover, and then you drop into the cloud bank from a high altitude and then down into the target zone."

"You see what I'm getting at?" Soren addressed everyone, but his eyes were fastened on Gylfie. "We've got a front coming in tonight. As a matter of fact, it's going to be miserable. Drenching rains, thick oily clouds, sooty as a forest fire — with sleet and all sorts of mess.

If we dropped three owls into the Palace of Mists with coals, bonk coals . . ."

"What?" Bubo said. "I mean, you're welcome to any bonks from my forge, but why?" Then the light began to twinkle in the Great Horned's amber eyes. "Oh! I get it! The old shell game!"

"Precisely!" Soren said. "Who has the Ember of Hoole? When these three owls fly out, each one will be carrying botkins, each botkin filled with several bonk embers. As we know, bonk coals are nearly indistinguishable from the true Ember of Hoole. It takes a careful eye to detect the true ember." He glanced over at Bubo who, indeed, had such an eye. "So who's to know which owl has the real Ember of Hoole?"

"Brilliant!" Digger exclaimed. "But a note of caution here. These owls should not be — well, how should I put it? High-profile owls."

"In other words, not the Band," Otulissa said.

"Yes," Soren replied. "Not the Band, and certainly not Coryn." He paused. "But there is another suggestion that I would like to make. None of the three, nor any of us, for that matter, should know who carries the true ember."

"Why?" Twilight said.

"These are young owls. We don't know how they'll conduct themselves if captured, for one thing. But more important, it is always better in a situation like this if the main operatives do not have the full story. Divide up the information, so to speak, and then there is less to divulge. It's a security measure. If, and for now let's call him or her Owl X, is captured, and the captors demand the ember, Owl X can say, 'I'm not sure if I have the ember. Several owls were sent out, only one has the real ember.'"

"Ingenious!" Digger exclaimed. "That will throw them off their game."

"That's the idea," Soren replied.

"Now." Digger stepped forward. "It is my feeling that Owl X and Owl Y and Owl Z should all be owls that are double chawed."

Double chawed was a term used for those young owls bright enough and talented enough to be assigned to two chaws. Soren and Otulissa had been double chawed when they were young.

"Well, there are Fritha and Wensel," Otulissa offered. "They are both very reliable."

"I wish we could send a third owl who is older to look out for them," Soren said. "You know, someone really experienced."

"What about Ruby?" Coryn said. "She's r
low-profile, but she's not as well known as the
she is the best flier in the tree."

"But wouldn't she be recognized?" Twilight said. "I mean, all those ruddy feathers."

"Not if you dipped her in a bit of bingle juice mixed with ground pellets." It was Octavia who spoke, the ancient, portly nest-maid snake. She had slithered into the hollow unnoticed.

"What?" several of the owls blurted out.

Cleve cocked his head. "Yes, of course. I've heard of this. It's a dye. It is also used in a very diluted form for gizzard mites. Provokes yarping."

"Are you saying, Octavia," Soren swiveled his head toward the old nest-maid snake who had spiraled herself into a plump coil in the middle of the hollow, "that Ruby could dye her plumage a different color?"

"Yes, then she wouldn't be recognized." She paused. "At least not by her feathers. Perhaps her flying style might give her away."

"Interesting idea," Digger said.

Soren turned toward Digger. "I think that it is a very good idea. We have Fritha and Wensel, extremely talented. Fritha, a little older, a bit more experienced. But Wensel is fantastic in all sorts of weather conditions.

and he has an artist's imagination. Somehow, I think we'll need someone like Wensel."

"Where does art comes into it?" Twilight said gruffly.

Gylfie snapped, "You were just talking about the artistry of Bess sending that owl to hagsmire instead of glaumora."

"Oh, so I was." Twilight blinked.

"And so it is decided. Fritha, Wensel, and Ruby will be the three owls to fly to the Palace of Mists and initiate the shell game," Soren said, turning to Coryn.

Coryn nodded. "And now the question is, where are they to take the ember?"

"Before we get to that," Soren said, "there is one more part to the plan. If these three owls are followed by anyone, we want to know who that is. The beauty of the weather that I see setting in is that it will allow the perfect cloud cover for the HALO drop not only for the three owls but for us, as well."

"For us?" Twilight asked.

"I want to be buried in that cloud cover and track our three ember-carrying owls and anyone else who is following them."

"But if it's a cloud cover, how will you see?" But

as soon as Twilight asked the question, he knew the answer.

"I'll *hear*!" Soren said.

Of course, for Soren was a Barn Owl. A Barn Owl's auditory skills were unmatched by any other species of owl. "I can recognize Nyra's wing beats. How many times have we battled these owls?"

"Too many," Digger sighed.

"But I'll need at least two more Barn Owls. I was thinking of Eglantine and Fiona. Fiona is young, but her hearing is extraordinary even for a Barn Owl."

"And now to what I feel is the most important question. Where are they to take the ember?" Everyone's head swiveled toward Coryn. As the anointed king, the embered monarch of the owl kingdoms, he was the only one who could make this decision. There was a long pause before he spoke. Finally, he said, "I have been thinking about this question ever since we started talking about this shell game." *Indeed,* he thought to himself, *I have been pondering this question longer than you can imagine.* "It seems to me," he continued, "that if the three owls succeed in getting the ember out, we should take it far away." Coryn now looked at Tengshu, who had been perched quietly in a shadowy corner of the hollow. "To the Middle Kingdom . . . to the Mountain of Time."

"I am not sure, Coryn," Tengshu said. "You understand that the ember is . . . is . . ." He hesitated. "A powerful relic from the ancient world."

"Yes," Coryn agreed. "Theo fought beside Hoole when he first dived into the flames of Dunmore to retrieve it. It is a most vital link between not only the time of legends and now, but between our kingdom and yours, the Middle Kingdom, for Theo found his way there, Tengshu."

There was much more that Coryn was considering and chose not to say. Theo had been a gizzard-resister. After his service to King Hoole, he had flown as far away as he could from the violence of his world — to the Middle Kingdom. In many respects, Coryn felt the same way about the Ember of Hoole that Theo felt about battle claws. He, however, was king, so he could not leave. But he could send this ember to the farthest reaches of the owl world — to the Middle Kingdom.

Soren regarded his nephew closely. *He wants to be rid of that ember so badly. And yet he is king.* It was astute of Coryn to link the ember to Theo, Soren thought.

Tengshu blinked. "I must go and ask the H'ryth if this is possible, if he will accept the ember."

"Could you leave soon?" Coryn asked.

"Yes, I shall leave immediately."

"And I shall speak to Ruby, Fritha, and Wensel," Otulissa said.

"Uh . . . Please stay, Otulissa.'" Soren hesitated before he began to speak. He coughed. "Perhaps Bubo, Twilight, Digger, and Gylfie could go and talk to Ruby, Fritha, and Wensel."

The owls looked at Soren, bewildered.

"There is another item that we must focus on."

"Indeed, the rumors of hagsfiends!" Coryn whispered.

"We hope they are rumors," Soren said. "But not only that. What of this sighting of the Striga and Nyra together in the Northern Kingdoms? It must be investigated immediately. I want to talk to Otulissa and Cleve about a reconnaissance mission to the Northern Kingdoms." Otulissa seemed to grow larger. Her plumage billowed. This was the first time she had been asked to do anything of import since her grave injuries. Tengshu, who had just been leaving the hollow, stopped. He swiveled his head toward Cleve and blinked. Cleve blinked back. Everyone's attention was focused on Soren, who had begun to speak.

No one noticed the quick exchange between Tengshu and Cleve, except one bird — the puffin. *I wonder what that's all about?* Dumpy thought. *I'm not that bright, but something was said without words. A signal. I'd bet my wee brain on it.*

Soren continued. "And I want to set up a crack corps of messengers to fly between all the Guardians on this mission, to deliver word of progress or problems. So when you're finished speaking with Fritha, Wensel, and Ruby, come back here. There's more to plan."

Half an hour later, Twilight, Gylfie, Digger, and Bubo returned. Soren looked up. "We're just finishing."

"Good," Coryn said. "Now we're all here." He looked at his uncle. "Soren, catch them up."

Soren swiveled his head toward Otulissa. "Otulissa will go to the Northern Kingdoms with Cleve." He explained the reconnaissance mission that was planned for them. They were to talk to as many animals as they could, including gadfeathers and even kraals, if it was safe, and polar bears as well, to find out if there had been any sightings of a blue owl and a haggish-looking Barn Owl. "And," he added in a low voice, "if there are any signs of strange-looking eggs.

"In addition to that, we have discussed the corps of messengers. It is to be headed by Martin, along with Nut Beam, Silver, Primrose, and Clover." Clover was a

Barn Owl. It was always wise to have one Barn Owl in any unit because of their auditory skills. They were all good owls, fast fliers, and fearless.

"Let us call this crack messenger unit the Joss Corps." Coryn spoke as he peered into the grate of the fire without turning around. Soren looked at the broad back of his nephew. Joss was the famous messenger from the time of the legends, the time of Hoole and Theo. *What exactly is Coryn thinking about? Yes, we are confronting a horrendous possibility, but there is more to it for him than what he is letting on,* Soren thought. *We all know what is at stake, but there is something even beyond that for Coryn.*

Coryn continued to peer into the grate and study the flames. Coryn was a flame reader and it was just a year ago that he had detected the ice-bright cave with the two shadowy figures in the flames. He had suspected that the huddled shapes were his mother and the Striga. But such flame readings were rarely precise, and never yielded complete information. Like encounters with scrooms, they often raised more questions than they answered. But now as he looked into the flames, he saw the figures of seven owls. One was far to starboard and another was lower in the plane, but five in the center flew close.

Coryn turned and said quietly, "The Chaw of Chaws. They will be the gizzard of this Operation HALO."

Soren returned to his own hollow. A milky light, the first streaks of dawn, washed into the cozy space. Pelli and the three B's were already sound asleep. He gazed down at them. *If the Striga and Nyra prevailed* . . . He tried to cut off the thought, the unthinkable image of those two. So much to lose. "Too many," Digger had replied when Soren had asked rhetorically how many times they had fought the Pure Ones. Most of his life, even his childhood, had been involved with fighting them. Soren's mind ranged back. The first fight had been the rescue of dear Ezylryb from the Devil's Triangle. But there had been so many after that.

He looked over at the newest-model battle claws that Quentin the quartermaster had just delivered — double-hinged retractables, or DHRs. Absolutely lethal. Would these improve his chances in battle? He tried them on. They were light, he would give them that. Maneuvering would be easy. But were they too light? The younger owls could adapt to these things. He was used to weight. He looked up on the wall of the hollow where the old battle claws hung that Ezylryb had given him. Now those were battle claws with heft! And they'd gotten him through . . . how many battles? Too many! *But there is another to come,* Soren thought, then whispered, "Another to come." He took off the new battle claws and reached for those of his old mentor. *Real antiques,* he thought. *But they're battle tested. They worked for Ezylryb and they'll work for me, Glaux willing.*

CHAPTER TEN

# A Dreadful Mis-hatch!

Dumpy had guided Otulissa and Cleve to the back entrance of the cave in the Ice Narrows. They perched on the ice cliff high above the cave's entrance, to say good-bye to the puffin.

"You have been more help than you'll ever know," Otulissa told him. "You were brave and smart. Now on your way," she said. "We'll send one of the Jossian messengers if we need to get in touch with you."

Otulissa and Cleve found the niche that opened into the cave. She slipped into the crack first and peered around. It appeared to be vacant. She had expected as much. A full moon cycle had passed since Dumpy had seen the Striga and Nyra there. "Nothing." She swiveled her head and whispered over her shoulder to Cleve, "But we should still look around. We might find clues of some sort." So they squeezed through the crack into the larger space of the cave. It hadn't been half a minute before Cleve exclaimed, "Yes, clues like this!" He held up a sapphire-blue feather. "The Striga's?"

Otulissa flew closer and squinted with her only eye. "Oh, dear!" she said softly. Cleve was confused. Otulissa sounded disappointed. "It's blue, but unfortunately it's not turquoise enough; it's not the Striga's, but that of another blue owl!"

"You're saying that there might be more blue owls involved?" Cleve asked hesitantly.

Otulissa nodded. "On my visit to the Middle Kingdom I noticed that the owls were not all the same shade of blue. Their plumage varied from turquoise to sapphire to emerald. The Striga's feathers are definitely in the turquoise range. You might have noticed that Tengshu's tend more toward cobalt."

"You think another owl from the Middle Kingdom has come here?"

"I fear so." Then the Spotted Owl's single eye seemed to focus on something. "What's that?" she exclaimed. She rushed to a corner of the ice cave. From behind, Cleve saw her wilf.

"Otulissa, dear, what is it?" He rushed to her side and looked down. "Oh, no!" They were both transfixed by the fragments of the shell of a dark and peculiar egg. There was a smear on the ice of some viscous fluid — now frozen — and close by lay a pulpy mass. Otulissa bent closer.

"Something nearly came to life here — then failed." Otulissa's voice trembled. Although the remnants were frozen, a rank odor hung in the air above the mess. "A mis-hatch."

"But not just any mis-hatch," Cleve said. He had taken a sliver of ice and was poking at the half-frozen blob on the floor of the cave.

"Incipient beak," Otulissa murmured.

"Some embryonic feather shafts, rather long," Cleve whispered.

"Some ocular cells — but such a bright yellow!" Otulissa's voice registered shock.

Otulissa turned slowly toward Cleve. "You're right. No ordinary mis-hatch. It was to be a hagsfiend! But something scared the 'mother' off, if whatever brooded over such an egg can be called a mother. She tried to escape with the egg but it broke."

"Let's hope this was the only egg," Cleve said.

"Well, I don't think we can be sure. They might have rescued others."

"Where would they have taken them, though?" Cleve asked.

"Perhaps to the old Ice Cliff Palace where Siv took the egg of Hoole." Otulissa spoke in an almost trance-like voice. "Just like in the legends."

"Surely they would not know about that, Otulissa," Cleve said.

"Why not? You forget that at one time, before we knew how terrible the Striga was, he had Coryn's confidence and the run of our library. They spent long evenings together. Coryn could have told him the stories of the legends. Siv finding refuge in the Ice Cliff Palace with her egg and her faithful servant, Myrrthe. It was all written down in the first legend by Grank."

"Of course," Cleve replied in a low tremulous voice. "Grank, the first collier."

"And as far as the *Book of Kreeth,* well, I said that I had the book under lock and key, but who knows — perhaps Coryn was reading it and the Striga glanced at it. And for a brief time before the Battle of the Book, it was in Nyra's possession."

"We have to get a message back to the great tree and inform them of what we have found."

There was a Jossian unit messenger stationed on the Ice Dagger. Otulissa and Cleve left immediately to report this latest and most dire news.

CHAPTER ELEVEN

# Stirrings in the Dragon Court

Far away, in the Middle Kingdom of Jouzhenkyn, Taya, a blue owl who served as a page in the Dragon Court of the Panqua Palace, was troubled. She had been a page for perhaps one hundred years and recently had detected currents of — for lack of a better word — energy among the court owls. She had never before felt such currents there. Was it restlessness? Such disquiet was almost unimaginable amid the thick lethargy of the Dragon Court owls. Their vanity linked with their dullness of wit had kept them subdued. The excessive pride they took in their plumage had led them to grow their feathers to such extravagant lengths that they could hardly fly, and for the most part were towed about the jeweled interior of the palace by bearers. There had been the unfortunate incident of Orlando, who had managed to pluck his feathers secretly until they were a reasonable length for flight and then escaped. How he had ever managed to learn how to fly was still a mystery. But as far as Taya knew, the other owls of the Dragon Court were too listless to have even noticed.

Taya had detected this strange energy perhaps two or three moon cycles previously. At first, she thought it was her imagination. But now she began to wonder again when she saw two azure-colored owls whispering with a new brightness in their eyes. She watched carefully as they were towed side by side through the Hollow of Benevolence and Forgiveness in the wake of the Empress Dowager. The empress seemed as dull-eyed as ever. Taya sensed an impatience in the two azure owls, as if they wanted to move faster. This was unheard of. Taya also observed that their feathers seemed somehow different. She decided she had to discuss her concerns with the steward. A pompous old owl, he was only the third steward since the creation of the Panqua Palace nearly one thousand years before by Theosang, the first H'ryth. Taya was not looking forward to this meeting but it needed to be done. She proceeded toward his office, the Jasper Chamber directly off the Hollow of Perpetual Beauty, where the dragon owls indulged in endless preening.

"Permission to see the steward." Taya addressed a tiny cerulean-blue owl, who resembled an Elf Owl except for his color.

"Do you have an appointment?"

"No, but this is important."

"That's what they all say." He had mastered the cultivated weariness of the steward's many sycophants. They all tried to lord their position over the other owls who served in the Panqua Palace. One had to play their game, had to toady up to them the way they toadied to the steward. The cerulean owl named Pingong would take a bit of work.

"Come on, Ping. You know I hardly ever ask for an audience with the steward," Taya said. Pingong gave Taya a look of disdain which was not easy since she towered over him. *How does an owl who is one-third my height manage to look down at me?* Taya wondered. She was becoming tired of this game. What she had to talk to the steward about was important and she was getting very irritated. "Look," Taya said. "The last secretary to the steward was let go because the head page complained. That was maybe fifty years ago, and guess what? I'm the head page now. If you consult the Panqua Scroll of Peerage, in the staffing section for the palace, you will find that I actually outrank you." The little owl wilfed a bit and became slightly smaller. "So let's be reasonable."

"Oh, all right. He's in there now, going over the menus."

The steward was a jade-blue with dashes of a softer blue in his coverts. He was bent over some charts. "Yes," he said, but did not look up.

"High Steward," Taya began. No one was ever allowed to address the steward by anything but his title, never his name. "I have recently become aware of a stirring, a suspicious energy in the palace."

The steward still did not look up. This was part of his game. It did not disturb Taya in the least. She was about to go on when he said, "Are you aware, Taya, that this new source of yak butter I found for the preening has not only increased the dragon owls' feather growth, but since we have incorporated it into their diet, it seems to be making them even fatter and slower. They delight in it."

Yak butter was the fuel used for fire in the Middle Kingdom. Every hollow had its yak butter lamps. It was rarely used for feather conditioner. *And,* thought Taya, *I am sure you're getting a kickback.*

The high steward could be absolutely maddening.

"Look," Taya said impatiently. "With all due respect, I did not come here to talk about yak butter."

Now the jade-blue owl looked up from his scroll. "I don't care for your tone, Taya," he said slowly.

Taya ignored the comment and barged ahead. "I'm worried. I am detecting unrest."

"You have a very active imagination."

"Before Orlando left . . ."

The high steward cut her off immediately. "We don't speak of that. It was a freakish anomaly."

"Indeed!" Taya said pointedly, and glared at the high steward, her contempt barely concealed. "When was the last time we took a census?"

"A census? You mean, actually counting all the owls in the Panqua Palace?"

"Yes, this used to be done on a regular basis."

"It was found to be a waste of time and effort. There are more than a thousand owls here."

"Are there?" Taya said softly. The jade-blue owl puffed up his feathers. He narrowed his eyes. As if to say, *You dare challenge me?* But instead, he returned to his study of the fat content in yak milk. "You are dismissed, Taya. Do not bother me again with your imaginative ramblings."

Taya whirled and flew out of the Jasper Chamber. She was absolutely furious. Tearing through the Hollow of Extended Preening and then taking a sharp turn, she swept down the Hollow of Supreme Contentment where the Empress Dowager was being towed by her servants. The wafting extravagance of her feathers created a soft weather of their own that actually generated thermals on which servants could often soar without stirring a wing. The empress tipped her head up. "Why the rush, dear Taya? Enjoy my thermal drafts."

"Yes, they are lovely, glorious. They wrap me in your eternal beauty and warmth."

It was part of court etiquette to answer almost any remark from one of the dragon owls with lavish praise. Taya knew that she must slow her flight or she would be in for yet another reprimand from the minister of protocol. Perhaps slowing down was good. It would give her time to think. Her emotions had gotten the better of her during the disastrous interview with the high steward. She would coast along for a bit and then discreetly leave the Empress Dowager's thermal wake at the Amethyst Gate.

Despite the spaciousness of the Panqua Palace's hollows and the dazzling beauty of its jeweled walls and pillars, there was not a servant who did not welcome a break from its splendor when they could fly freely outside, encountering the real wind and the tumultuous drafts that blew off the snowy peaks of the Middle Kingdom. Each servant earned a leave of absence, usually once a moon cycle, when they would return and visit their families. And although it was an honor to serve in the Panqua Palace, it was an even greater one to serve as pikyus, the spiritual teachers who resided in the owlery at the Mountain of Time. But few were qualified and even fewer were chosen for the long arduous course of study.

After leaving the dowager's procession, Taya had been riding some crisp drafts not far from the opening split of the enormous geode that formed the structure of the Panqua Palace, when she spied a small blue cyclonic swirl rising up as if directly through the walls of the geode. She immediately went into a steep, banking turn to investigate closer. *It must be from one of the vents,* she thought. There were a series of natural vents penetrating the geode that brought in thin rivulets of fresh air to the outermost walls and chambers of the palace. These chambers were used mostly for storage of yak butter and as servants' quarters. She alighted on a cornice just by the vent and poked her beak through.

She blinked and felt a stab deep in her gizzard. There was an enormous pile of blue feathers in the chamber. Many of them had broken and bloodied shafts. These had not been naturally molted at all, but unnaturally plucked. This was precisely how Orlando had succeeded in arresting the extreme growth of his feathers before making his escape. Plucking the feathers when they were at the proper stage encouraged vigorous growth, and kept the vain dragon owls earthbound, but plucking when they were freen inhibited this growth, which was exactly what Orlando did to get himself flight-ready. *How many Dragon Court owls are flight-ready right now?* Taya wondered.

She peered down at the pile of blood-streaked feathers. It seemed immense. Was a rebellion brewing? How many had already flown away, and where had they gone? She raged now when she thought of her curt dismissal by the high steward. He had nearly laughed at her when she had suggested a census. Then a maverick thought shot through her brain and she felt her gizzard freeze. Forget the dragon owl census. What about the sterile eggs that the dragon owls of the Panqua Palace routinely produced? Unlike most sterile eggs, these were not allowed to remain in a nest for five minutes but were immediately removed by servants and destroyed. They were smashed to bits for reasons never quite clear to Taya but in strict accordance with instructions explicitly laid down in the Theo Papers. Hadn't she noticed that the mound of broken eggshells that she often flew over seemed smaller of late?

Taya now flew to the far side of the cliffs, where the refuse heaps were. There were mounds of yarped pellets and knolls made from the smashed shells of the infertile eggs. She was about to fly closer to the eggshell mound when she noticed one of the lower-echelon owls of the preening unit. His beak was slick with yak butter and he was poking into the yarped pellet heap. Why would a preener be sticking his nose into yarped pellets? Were there ingredients for some kind of beauty treatment to be found? Hardly! The notion was disgusting and would certainly offend the vanity of any dragon owl worth its fancy plumage. Taya watched closely. Her eyes widened. She felt her gizzard clutch. He was arranging pellets carefully around something. What was it? *Why doesn't he leave?* She was desperate to see why a preener would be hanging around this offal. Finally, he left.

As soon as he was out of sight, Taya flew down. She looked about, then began to poke her beak into the area where she had seen the preener. Her beak struck something! With her talons, she began carefully picking off the top layer of pellets. When she got to the bottom of the pile of pellets, she noticed the ground had been recently disturbed. So she began scratching at the loose gravelly debris. Within half a minute she saw something all too familiar — the gleaming dark shell of a sterile dragon owl's egg. At that moment, Taya thought she might faint dead away. Her first instinct was to destroy it. But this had to be part of some terrible plot, a heinous conspiracy, and if the conspirators knew she was on to them, it would make it more difficult to catch them. She first had to tell someone. Not the steward, obviously. For all she knew, he was the owl behind the plot. No, there was only one thing to do.

She turned, spread her wings, and took off into a blast of cold air. Climbing over the blast with a fury, she began flying as fast as she had ever flown to the one place where she would be listened to: the owlery at the Mountain of Time. The H'ryth would hear her out. The H'ryth was the opposite of the high steward. Humble, meek, with a deep wisdom of the ages that sparkled like green glints in his pale yellow eyes. He was, after all, the direct spiritual descendant of the first H'ryth, Theosang.

## CHAPTER TWELVE

# "Glaux Speed!"

The rain was soft, slanting down from the clouds. Six owls had flown out of the great tree on a course due west across the Sea of Hoolemere. It was the Band, plus two Barn Owls, Soren's sister, Eglantine, and the young Fiona. They were flying high in the uppermost stria of clouds. The sharp tang of the Hoolemere Sea cut through the rain. "It must be wild down there," Twilight said.

It was beyond wild, Soren thought. He had never seen such weather. The dark, roiling clouds were perfect for their purposes and yet the tumult of the storm winds, which always thrilled him in the same way as they had his mentor Ezylryb, now seemed disturbing. He looked up at the nearly black clouds and imagined that they reflected an even greater storm to come.

Gylfie was navigating as usual. She now flew with a tiny device — a clock that was called a chronometer, which was based on an ancient instrument from the time of the Others, and consulted it often. She now gave a position report: "We are, to the best of my knowledge, over the Shadow Forest."

"The Shadow Forest must be getting hammered," Twilight said.

"Not many other owls would come out in this," Digger said.

"Let alone bury themselves in the upper cloud layer while three owls took care of business," Gylfie added with a churr. For that, indeed, was the plan that had been worked out in much greater detail since the first strategy session.

The Band, along with Eglantine and Fiona, were following Ruby, Wensel, and Fritha to the Palace of Mists. They would bury themselves in the stria just above the palace while the three owls collected the embers. When the three ember carriers departed the palace, they would take off in different directions and each would be covered by a pair of owls flying useen above them. One of each pair would be a Barn Owl who could track them, using its exceptional auditory skills, no matter what the weather. Each of the three ember carriers would ultimately arrive at the Wolf's Fang. The Wolf's Fang was a rock formation in the Sea of Vastness, which was a stopping point to the River of Wind that carried one to the Middle Kingdom. It was on this desolate sea-torn outpost that the ember carriers and their detail of trackers would rendezvous to await word from Tengshu to learn whether or not the H'ryth had given permission to transport the ember to the Middle Kingdom. At least that was the plan.

*I usually love flying this weather but this time it's not for fun,* Soren thought. *It's for the ember.* But then again, this weather was so Ezylryb! Below them the perfect storm was just getting organized. There was a kink in the usual weather patterns for this season. The katabats had begun to blow earlier than normal and an immense eddy from the River of Wind was billowing up in the far west. It blew at a high speed between the Hoolian world and that of the Middle Kingdom. Since Otulissa's injuries, Soren had been the primary researcher picking through the data they were gathering from the scores of feather buoys they had set out. Nights before, he had begun to get unusual readings. The calm sea was building into mountainous waves. They all heard an ominous whining periodically as the wind spiked to a new force. The keening wind was punctuated by the crashing of the towering waves onto the land below, uprooting entire sections of coastal forests.

As devastating as conditions were, they all added up to a perfect storm and, under its cover, the three owls, Fritha, Wensel, and Ruby, could take the ember out of the Palace of Mists and fly it as quickly as possible to the Middle Kingdom — if permission had been granted by the H'ryth.

Now in the dim light of the crypt at the Palace of Mists, Fritha, Ruby, and Wensel watched as Bess, with a set of pincers, drew out the teardrop-shaped cask that contained the ember. There was a prescribed manner in which the ember was to be deposited in one of the three botkins. Fritha, Ruby, and Wensel were to turn their tails so that they could not see which botkin Bess emptied the cask into. Each of the three botkins contained other bonk coals, which served two purposes: first to insulate the owls from the powerful effects of the ember, and second to camouflage the ember, which, to most, looked like any other bonk coal.

"All right, turn tail," Bess said quietly. The three owls turned around. There was no temptation to peek, although each owl did wonder if he or she would feel the presence of the true ember in the botkin. Fritha and Wensel were comparatively young owls and this was by far the most important mission they had been sent on since taking their oaths as Guardians. Fritha possessed a ferocity that belied her size. Wensel's personality was marked by the eccentricities and quirkiness associated with artists, for he was a gifted illustrator. He had an amazing capacity for coming up with creative solutions to almost any problem. Soren and Otulissa knew both of these owls well and felt they were perfect for the job. Ruby, of course, was Ruby. More experienced than either one of the others, she was arguably the finest flier in the entire tree. This was the best team for this mission.

Bess closed her own eyes and dropped the ember into one of the three botkins. It would be Bubo who would determine for sure which botkin had the ember when he met them at the Wolf's Fang with the other owls. And if the H'ryth agreed, it would be Tengshu who would carry the ember across the River of Wind to the Middle Kingdom.

With eyes still shut Bess then commenced to shuffle the containers around on the stone floor and then reshuffled them two more times. Opening her eyes, she said, "All right, go back to the position where your original botkin was." The owls did as they were told. She sighed deeply. "I guess that's it." They could hear the wind howling. It was so loud it nearly obliterated the crash of the waterfalls outside. It was an ominous, wild, keening sound. A shiver went through all of them.

"Sound of that wind gives me the creelies," Wensel said, and wrapped his wings around his chest as if to protect himself.

"Don't worry. That's the sound of a great wind for flying," Ruby said. "You'll get the ride of your life." Bess stole a glance a Ruby. No wonder Soren had sent Ruby. She was perfect for these young owls. She bolstered their spirits, supported them, encouraged them, and looked out for them. Ruby did, however, look different. After three dippings in the bingle juice mixture, Ruby's ruddy feathers were now a tawny blondish hue. No one would recognize her. Indeed, the only thing that might give her away was her skillful flying. But they hoped no owls would be out in this weather to see it.

"All right," Ruby said, taking a step closer to the others. "You've studied the charts. You each know your individual flight plan."

"Yes," Fritha answered. "I am to go due east from here into the canyonlands, then circle back west and head for Beyond the Beyond, and head straight out toward the Wolf's Fang."

"And you, Wensel?"

"Yes ma'am." Wensel then repeated the details of his route.

“Excellent!” Bess replied after they had recited their individual flight plans. She accompanied them to the turret opposite the bell tower and watched them take off into the wildness of the storm. She had to wedge herself into one of the stone turret notches to keep from being swept off. The raging wind blew the cascading water of the falls in horizontal sheets across the night. Trees shuddered, the noise of their branches a drumbeat beneath the wind. Flashes of lightning illuminated the undersides of rolling clouds, giving them a harsh metallic glow, and always that odd whining that sliced through the wind’s roar, splitting it like a talon through tender flesh.

But the three owls were amazing fliers. Bess watched as they lifted off into the teeth of the storm. Catching every favorable draft, they manipulated their wings constantly to adjust to the confusing air currents. There were alarming shifts and abrupt shears where a wind could accelerate or decelerate dramatically, change its direction completely, pocking the air with deadfalls and suck-down vents, which could spell disaster for the average flier. But these were no average fliers. “Glaux speed,” she murmured softly as she saw them dissolve into a thick dark cloud bank. “Glaux speed!”

CHAPTER THIRTEEN

# *Proposal or Experiment?*

In the Northern Kingdoms, there is a promontory that juts out into the Everwinter Sea, which is called the Ice Talons. On the southwest side of the Ice Talons, a thread of water penetrates deep into the interior of that frozen landscape and, on either side, spires of ice, twisted and turned by time and wind, rise wraithlike in the fog-shrouded air of that canyon. The spires are connected by ice bridges and arches and behind the walls of the canyon winds a complex maze of tunnels and channels. In ancient times, during a series of desperate wars, it had served as a stronghold, a hidden redoubt for the H'rathian monarchs, and upon one occasion, the widowed queen Siv had come here with her faithful servant, Myrrthe. With them they brought the egg from which the greatest of all kings would hatch: King Hoole, the first holder of the ember.

The canyon was, however, also known to be a passageway in ancient times, a shortcut for hagsfiends, who were said to have a refuge on the other side of the promontory, far from salt water. Hagsfiends liked to be as far from the ocean as possible. They feared salt water, for it destroyed their oil-less feathers, and, when drenched in briny water, they nearly always drowned instantly. They would rush through this narrow watery channel to get to dry land, hardly ever slowing to explore the tangled passageways of the cliffs.

And now two owls, who should have had no reason to fear water but were feeling nervous nonetheless, were making their way not to the dry land that had been the hagsfiends' redoubt — for they knew nothing of that place — but instead to another refuge deep within the ice cliffs. They carried in their botkins two dozen double- and triple-yolked eggs of monsters.

"Are you sure you know where we're going?" Nyra asked.

"Yes. Your son, Coryn, told me of this place. Or rather he read to me part of the legend of the first collier, which described it."

"His name is Nyroc. Not Coryn. I named him Nyroc. He ceased to be my son when he renamed himself Coryn. How far must we fly? Are you trying to find the exact spot where this ancient queen brought her egg?"

"Not the exact spot. Just a safe place for our experiments. And, even though many more eggs are coming, we can't afford to lose another one." He paused, then turned his head toward Nyra. "Everything has gone so well. Our troops in Kuneer are trained, organized. They will be ready to join us on Long Night. This is the last part of the plan, but the most important."

Nyra did not like the way the Striga had called them "*our* troops." She, in fact, was the one who had gathered the ragtag remnants of Pure Ones and rebuilt them into a fighting force. Yes, more troops had come and were coming to the Northern Kingdoms from the Dragon Court. But the backbone of this army, at present, was Pure Ones. However, she kept quiet about that. "We could have finished off those puffins that came looking for their brother in a snap," Nyra said. "Puffins are stupid. It would have been easy."

The Striga had to refrain from saying, "You're stupid." Instead, he replied, "Those puffins' bodies would have been discovered sooner or later. Rumors would start. It was better to get out as quickly as possible. We are just lucky that the one dragon owl got out with her botkin of eggs the night before."

"I suppose that's true. We didn't lose much. One egg went rolling into the water and another got smashed on the floor of the ice cave. But do you think that dragon owl who got out will find her way to the Ice Cliff Palace? What's her name?"

"Olong," the Striga said. "She is named for the color of her feathers. It means sapphire in our language. She's smart. She'll find her way. Now try not to worry. Many of these eggs are double- and triple-yolked. This is our starter batch. The converts are bringing in more." The "converts" were those Dragon Court owls who had surreptitiously been learning to fly and, one by one, or, on rare occasions, two by two, had been leaving the Panqua Palace. With the help of corrupt servants they were purloining eggs and bringing them to the Northern Kingdoms. Until now they had been stashing them in the most remote regions, inhabited, if at all, by the pirate owls, the kraals, who most other creatures tried to avoid. The eggs were sterile when they had been imported from the Middle Kingdom, but with proper brooding, unlike normal sterile eggs, they could be made to quicken and finally to hatch. This was part of the peculiar mystery, the terrible secret of a hagsfiend's genesis.

"And to think I nearly had my talons on that book. I had tried to read it but it was very hard to understand," Nyra whined.

"But you remembered some of it. And between us — look, Nyra! Look what we have already achieved. I should be pulling out my feathers in punishment, for the first time I ever heard Coryn mention the *Book of Kreeth,* I didn't have the wits to ask him more. I even got a glimpse of it one time in the library. You are indeed the better bird. You figured out its value."

If there was one thing the Striga knew, it was how to flatter. It was flattery that fueled the feckless life of the Dragon Court, and fawning adulation was its lifeblood.

The Striga thought back on that night when he had first glimpsed the *Book of Kreeth.* It seemed a lifetime ago. (Indeed, the blue owl was beginning to suspect that he had had many lifetimes. It was as if echoes from a long-forgotten past would sometimes reverberate through his brain.) On that particular night he now recalled that Otulissa had accidentally left a small cabinet in a back hollow of the library unlocked, and he had slipped into it to peek. What he found was a volume entitled the *Book of Kreeth,* and it puzzled him. It was mostly illustrations. But it made no sense whatsoever and he had thought the strange pictures were something to do with loathsome vanities. Just as well it be locked away. How stupid he had been!

At last the two owls with their precious cargo found a narrow opening in the ice cliffs. "I think this should do," the Striga said with relief.

"Is this the Ice Palace?" Nyra asked.

"I'm not sure if it is the Ice Palace proper. But I think we can be safe here. And now to construct a good schneddenfyrr," the Striga said.

"A schnedden . . . what?"

"A schneddenfyrr. It is an old Krakish word for 'ice nest.' That is what the owls of the Northern Kingdoms use because they lack trees, hence no tree hollows for eggs."

The Striga busied himself settling the eggs in ice nests. Nyra followed suit.

"You learned a lot," Nyra said.

"I learned it from your son and Otulissa and Soren. They aren't stupid, you know."

Nyra glared as he spoke.

"You must learn, Nyra dear, to use your enemies."

She did not like the intimacy of his tone. She was about to object but held her tongue. The Striga was right. One must learn to use one's enemies. And who knew, when the ember was hers, who her enemies might be? Perhaps the Striga! The dark, grayish eggs were the means to the ember. But the ember would only be possessed by one owl, and she planned to be that owl. So she would hold her tongue now and indulge this blue owl, who seemed to revel in these terms of endearment. A thought suddenly occurred to her — *Is he trying to woo me? Woo me as one would woo a mate?* Would she have shared the ember with her long-dead mate, Kludd, with whom she had brought that unruly son into the world? Once her gizzard had sung for dear Kludd. *But let's be practical. An ember cannot be divided,* she thought. And who would want to be queen to someone else's king when indeed she could be both king and queen?

She quietly observed the blue owl, who was fussing like an old nest-maid snake over this schnedden-whatever, arranging the eggs just so. He, too, seemed absorbed in private thoughts, but he now began to speak and what he said stirred something deep in Nyra. "Of course, you, of all owls, know of the curse of one who is hatched on the night of a lunar eclipse."

"I suppose," Nyra answered cagily, "that it depends on your viewpoint, whether it be a curse or not."

"True. Nevertheless, they say an enchantment is cast upon those hatchlings, a charm that leads to great power. Hoole was hatched on the night of a lunar eclipse. And he retrieved the ember for the first time."

"And so was my son," Nyra replied.

"And he became king, as well," the Striga said softly.

Nyra remembered the night. It was just after the end of the War of Fire and Ice, which was sometimes called the War of the Great Burning. She was soon lost in the reveries of that night Nyroc had hatched.

"Nyra, you are the one who explained to me that Kreeth was not only interested in creating strange monsters that were odd crossbreeds, but she had dabbled in creating a new strain of hagsfiends. You said they hatch from eggs such as these on the night of a lunar eclipse. Thanks to your diplomatic efforts with my brethren, the converts from the Panqua Palace, the eggs have been secured. Their contribution was great but yours is *immeasurable.* It was a setback when we were surprised in that cave in the Ice Narrows. But these eggs will be safe. The rest will be taken directly to the kraals' territory. The ice nests are readied. All we need to do is fetch those eggs and the broodies from the kraal region and lead them to the Ice Cliffs for the final days of brooding before the eclipse when the quickening begins. In all, we will have nearly one hundred eggs! A company! A company of hagsfiends!"

"I still don't see why we must quicken the eggs here. Why not leave them there in the kraals' territory?"

"Too exposed. The land is bare and windswept. These eggs need to be brooded out of the wind in proper schneddenfyrrs to quicken. No puffins here and no polar bears because the fishing is poor. But the old Ice Cliff Palace is the perfect place to brood these eggs. The broodies will sit on them, keep them warm, and so will we. We'll help them. But we must do this in shifts. For some of us must be ready to defend the eggs, in case there are intruders, like before. Soon it will be too late to move them."

"So you say." Nyra did not quite understand this, but she had agreed to it.

"Some say . . ." The Striga's voice seemed to creak as if he were carefully measuring the weight of each word. "Some say that we owls of the Dragon Court were once hagsfiends."

A charge shot through Nyra's gizzard like a bolt of lightning. The Striga continued. "That Theo created the court to disempower hagsfiends by smothering them in luxury and counterfeit power — to make us weak.

"Did it ever occur to you, Nyra, that you and I might share a heritage?"

Nyra blinked.

"Look at your feathers, my dear. Look how they have

darkened. See their ragged edges. You look no more like a Barn Owl than I do a Spotted Owl. We have lost our definition as an owl species."

*Where is he going with this talk?* Nyra wondered.

"Therefore," the Striga continued, "I think we might assume that we are on the brink of a new possibility." He glanced down fondly at the eggs, which seemed to have darkened in the few minutes since they had arrived. "Together we could realize this possibility."

"Together? Is this a proposal?"

"Let's just call it an experiment."

*How romantic!* Nyra thought derisively, but she held her tongue. He wanted to be her mate, yet she knew that ultimately this blue owl was her enemy.

CHAPTER FOURTEEN

# A Trace of Doubt

Coryn had not been idle since the Band had left and the mission to remove the ember from the Palace of Mists had commenced. Soren had devised an ingenious plan for dispatching the ember to the Middle Kingdom, if the H'ryth agreed. But Coryn needed to do more — he needed to devise a mighty strategy for smashing the combined forces of Nyra and the Striga, for those two were not settling down to raise a family but to conjure an army from hagsmire itself. So Coryn had plunged into reading every account he could find of past wars that the Guardians had fought. He analyzed battle strategies, the deployment of forces, and the use of NCWs — Non-Clawed Weaponry. He even reread the legends for the battle lore. Coryn sensed, as had Soren, that it was not a battle but a war they were heading into. *Yes, it would be wonderful if they could get the ember to safety. But what did that mean finally? Could the ember ever truly be safe? Unless . . .* He did not finish the thought.

He suddenly felt the need of company and summoned Mrs. Plithiver to his hollow.

"Ah, Mrs. P., good to see you," he said when she arrived.

"Always my pleasure, sir." She made a waggling little dip with her rose-colored head.

"Mrs. P., can I offer you some milkberry tea?"

"Oh no, sir. No, thank you." Mrs. Plithiver was an old-school nest-maid snake. She did not believe that servants should indulge in such liberties as dining at the same table as their masters and mistresses.

"You had something to discuss, sir?"

"Oh, Mrs. Plithiver, I wish you would just call me Coryn." It had taken Coryn forever to stop her from addressing him as "Your Majesty."

"Yes, Coryn." Just the manner in which she said his name made it sound like Your Majesty.

"Mrs. P., I have been reading Ezylryb's account of the War of Fire and Ice. I found the part about owlipoppen and how they were used to dupe the enemy amazing."

"Yes, very effective, sir . . . I mean, Coryn."

"I was wondering how they ever made so many of the little dolls."

"Oh, it was Audrey's doing. She is head of the weavers' guild, although all of us helped out."

They sipped tea in silence for some minutes. Mrs. P. sensed that he simply needed quiet company and his talk of owlipoppen was of no import. She saw him glance more than once at the flames in his grate.

A small thrill went though Mrs. P. when she realized her company was essential to him. She had worried that when the others had gone off he might feel left behind and sink into the gollymopes. Coryn was an owl whose gizzard had a melancholy turn. Mrs. P., like all blind nest-maid snakes, had developed her other sensibilities to a level of extreme refinement, and she was relieved to detect in Coryn no melancholy at all during the last few nights, but a new energy, a concentration, and a resolve. And yet, did she not sense just now, as she slithered from the hollow while Coryn stepped over to poke the fire in the grate, a trace of doubt hovering somewhere in his gizzard?

Small flames leaped up, casting shadows throughout the hollow, but Coryn kept his eyes focused on the rich central planes of one flame in particular. He knew he would not find any answers to his questions. The flames rarely yielded definitive answers. They could only suggest possibilities: truths, but confusing ones. He remembered his very first experiences in looking into a fire and realizing that there was some kind of meaning hidden there. It was in the flames over his father's bones that he had first seen the shape and the flickering colors of the Ember of Hoole. Of course, at the time he did not know the meaning of what he'd seen. But later those same flames revealed a truth he half suspected — that his father, Kludd, had not been murdered savagely by Soren, as his mother had told him, but had fallen in battle, and that Twilight had delivered the fatal wound in a war that was entirely the fault of the Pure Ones. Nyra had told him nothing but lies — lies about his father, lies about the Pure Ones, and most of all, lies about his uncle and the Guardians of Ga'Hoole. Now, as he stared into the fire once again, he knew he was looking for simple answers to questions he could not help asking. *What,* he thought, *shall I do if the H'ryth refuses to let us bring the ember to the owlery at the Mountain of Time? What then?*

# CHAPTER FIFTEEN
# Splendid Isolation – No More!

"You expect us to give refuge to this ember?"

Tengshu had never seen the H'ryth in such a rage. The stream of green light flowing from his eyes, which signified deep wisdom, had intensified. "Do you know what has happened since you've been gone? What I have just this morning been informed of?" The plumage on the H'ryth's head had been closely clipped except for the single blue feather that stood straight up. This was the identifying mark of all spiritual guides, the pikyus in the owlery. The feather quivered with his rage.

"No, honorable Gup Theosang. Enlighten me."

"An alert page from the Dragon Court has just discovered that a score of owls has fled."

"What?" Tengshu felt a quaking deep in his gizzard.

"They used the same strategy as the perfidious Orlando." The H'ryth's voice, which was usually smooth, was rasping.

"Self de-featheration?"

"Yes, and undoubtedly there were some accomplices. Two, possibly three, lower-echelon servants have gone with them."

Tengshu was aghast. He closed his eyes. "I am deeply sorry. I should not have abandoned my post at the Wind's Gates."

Gup Theosang's wings sagged a bit as he perched on the branch of petrified wood in the hollow at the very highest point in the Mountain of Time, a place known as the Hollow of Supreme Concentration. "It is not your fault. They would have found some other route to the River of Wind."

"Perhaps, but my qui lines might have detected their track, some remnant feather from their flight."

Gup Theosang was an owl of great empathy. "I do not need you wallowing in remorse. I need your brain, Tengshu. You are a sage. These owls undoubtedly will join Orlando, who now calls himself 'the Striga' as I understand. There is no telling what they will do. But eventually they will come back here and wreak havoc. We must prepare. I knew it was a bad thing when the

Guardians came here. For more than a thousand years we had lived untouched by owls from any other worlds, kingdoms. Splendid isolation!"

*He calls it "splendid," this isolation,* Tengshu thought. *But one cannot live like that forever.* It was too late now. They had a responsibility to help the Hoolian owls. They could no longer indulge in this so-called "splendid isolation." Although for years, Tengshu, who was also known as the Sage of the River's End, had led a hermetic life, he was more cognizant and versed in the wider flow of life than one might imagine. He was wise, but he was also politic. With subtlety, he could steer owls not toward his own purposes, but better purposes. He intended to do that now with Gup Theosang, the H'ryth. But unlike the Striga, he did not manipulate through falseness or flattery but directed through clarity and honesty.

"Gup Theosang, you are right. The Ember of Hoole has no place in here. It will put us at great risk. It will put in greater jeopardy any hope for isolation of our Middle Kingdom, an isolation that we have valued for centuries."

"I am glad you see my reason." The H'ryth nodded.

"I do. I do indeed. But I also see that the seal of our kingdom has been broken. For almost one thousand years, the Hoolian world did not know that we existed.

Although by the grace of our first H'ryth, Theo, we knew of them."

"He knew that if they knew of us, ultimately there would be fighting. He taught us the Way of Gentleness because he so hated the weapons that he had made as a . . . what do they call them? I cannot even remember the dreadful term."

"Blacksmith."

"Yes, blacksmith. And already we have seen a battle using these vile weapons in our own air, our own sky."

*But what the H'ryth does not understand,* Tengshu thought, *is that there is no such thing as "our own sky," or "our own air." The sky is the very thing, the entity, the reality that connects us all, no matter if we are Hoolian or Jouzhen owls.*

Tengshu continued. "And there could be more fighting, Gup Theosang. The tyrannical owls, who called themselves the Pure Ones, chased the Guardians here. But we know from Theo and the Theo Papers that the Guardians are good owls, noble owls. Now you must realize that Orlando and the Dragon Court owls who have fled to the Hoolian kingdoms will join forces with these so-called Pure Ones. You see, it is the Pure Ones who want the ember, and so does Orlando. If that ember falls into the wrong talons, it will be catastrophic for all owls no matter where they live — here or in the Hoolian world."

"You cannot be sure the dragon owls who just fled will join Orlando and these Pure Ones. Or, for that matter, if Orlando will join the Pure Ones." There was a note of desperation in the H'ryth's voice.

"Gup Theosang, Orlando already has joined the Pure Ones."

"What?" The H'ryth staggered on his perch. "You know this with certainty?"

"Yes, with absolute certainty. Reports from trusted sources — sources too . . . simple to lie — put Orlando and the owl called Nyra, leader of the Pure Ones, together." He waited a moment. The green light that flowed from the H'ryth's eyes seemed to congeal. "Not only that. There are rumors about eggs — strange eggs." He remembered Dumpy's reconstruction of the conversation he had overheard between the Striga and Nyra.

The H'ryth gasped in alarm. "This is bad. Terrible! You remember the middle chapters of the papers of Theo?"

Tengshu nodded solemnly. "I do indeed! In the Theo Papers there was a section pertaining to the reproductive habits of the Dragon Court owls. It was theorized that if these owls' feathers were allowed to grow to extravagant lengths they would no longer be able of produce offspring. It would effectively terminate egg laying. And the eggs these Dragon Court owls had laid prior to the therapies to stimulate feather growth had been extremely strange in color. Not white and spherical like all owl eggs, but gray that would darken to black. And they were often oddly shaped."

"Tengshu, this can't be!"

"I'm afraid it is true, and then where are we?"

"Then we stand in grave danger of violating our Theotic Oath." The Theotic Oath was the vow to Theo in which the owls of the Mountain of Time swore to maintain the Dragon Court forever in the ways prescribed by the revered Theosang, the first H'ryth. "What do you propose, Tengshu?"

"I propose we do exactly as you have suggested. We should not agree to provide a refuge for the Ember of Hoole." This much had become very clear to Tengshu. It was the Hoolian ember. It had no business being out of the five kingdoms at the other end of the River of Wind. But at the same time, the Hoolian world needed their help. Help to vanquish once and for all these maniacal owls, now reinforced with recruits from their own Middle Kingdom. He took a step closer to Gup Theosang. "But sir, we should not deceive ourselves. We can avoid the ember, but we cannot avoid the battle, nay, the *war* that will inevitably come. The survival of the civilized kingdoms of good owls depends upon the outcome of this conflict. The fury and the might of these evil owls and their forces could easily be turned on us, our own Jouzhen empire invaded. If we fail, the world of owls will sink into an abyss of darkness and the most sinister epoch imaginable will commence. I am asking for an entire Danyar division. We must fly across the River of Wind to the Hoolian Kingdoms. And fight!"

This was going to be a massive war. It would require immense power. This would be the War of the Ember.

## CHAPTER SIXTEEN

# To the Northern Kingdoms

Though Otulissa had never been a member of the tracking or search-and-rescue chaws, she had a sixth sense about certain things beyond her expertise. This sense began to stir in her gizzard. Shortly before she and Cleve had left Dumpy off in the Ice Narrows, Otulissa had warned Dumpy to say nothing but to keep his eyes wide open, and if he saw anything alarming, he was to fly immediately to Nut Beam, one of the Jossian messengers who had been installed at Coryn's command on the Ice Dagger. Nut Beam would then get word to the Guardians.

Otulissa and Cleve had been holding fast to a north by northeast course. The wind was hard on them, but soon they would be inside the protection of the Ice Talons. There was a momentary lull in the wind and then the rain came down harder, denting the surface of the water below. Otulissa's sixth sense twisted her gizzard painfully and she took a sudden dive.

"What are you doing?" Cleve called out as he watched her veer off the shoulder of the headwind.

"Course change!" she shouted back urgently. Now she was carving a turn that put them on a due east heading. Otulissa was hovering over a swirl of water. Laced in its foamy frills were feathers — blue feathers. Some pale, some the blue of midnight, some the tint of sapphires. None, however, were the turquoise of the Striga's feathers. "This looks like a reverse eddy," she said. "They sometimes occur spontaneously near land formations like this." She indicated with her head the long reach of coastline to one side and the easternmost claw of the Ice Talons. "They begin at the head of the narrow inlet far inland and eventually spin their way to sea, catching bits of airborne flotsam as they go."

"Such as blue feathers," Cleve replied. Then like the blare of an alarm, "Otulissa!" Cleve hovered just inches over the swirling feathers.

"What is it, Cleve?"

"There aren't just blue feathers here. Some are painted bright pink. And look — blood! There's been a fight near here." Cleve tried to quell the rising panic he felt. If there were wounded owls, he needed to help them. This was his duty. Cleve was a healer. He turned to Otulissa. "We need to think this through. It's a short distance to the shore. We can get out of the wind under the rocks there."

A few minutes later, the two owls huddled on a small scrap of beach under a rocky overhang. They had plucked the mass of feathers from the water so they could examine them more closely. There were several kraal feathers stained with blood. "Broken shafts!" Cleve said. "This was a real battle."

"And then there are the emerald and cobalt-blue ones," Otulissa said.

"Yes, but those aren't broken. I'd wager the blue owls won." Then he inhaled sharply. "That's not a kraal feather or one from a blue owl." He picked up a creamy white feather, a primary from a Snowy Owl, by the look of it, the bottom portion of which was soaked in blood. A few red berries still clung to it. "That's a gadfeather's," he said.

"A gadfeather's!" Otulissa said, shocked. "Gadfeathers just sing. They are peace-loving. Kraals fighting is one thing, but gadfeathers? Are you sure it's a gadfeather's? I mean, there are lots of Snowy Owls up here and not all are gadfeathers."

"There are bright berries, here, in the blood. And I know of only one gadfeather in the Northern

Kingdom whose plumage is this creamy color. Isa!" Cleve whispered.

Otulissa wilfed. She had heard Cleve speak of Isa. Her singing voice was renowned. At one point, Otulissa had wondered if Cleve had not once been the tiniest bit in love with Isa.

"We are not far from kraal territory here," Otulissa said. "Straight inland there is a place called the Gray Rocks. Poor ice there, but the kraals like it. There are no firths, no fingers of water penetrating the territory. It is deep inland. Bushes grow there from which they harvest special berries for their dyes." She paused. "It was also," she spoke slowly, "a favorite place for hagsfiends. At least in the time of the legends. But why would it be favored now?" she asked in a professorial manner. Otulissa had begun pacing up and down under the overhang, her wings tucked neatly behind her so that the edges of the primaries interlocked in a seam down the middle of her back. "Yes, we must ask ourselves why they would go there. True, it is far from salt water, which hagsfiends feared. But why are the blue owls so fearful? It is very hard to make a traditional schneddenfyrr in that region, for there is little ice. They must seek this place for its remoteness and . . . and . . ." Otulissa's single eye began to sparkle. "Of course, how easy it would be for an owl of such plumage" — she held up the cobalt blue feather — "to blend in with those gaudy kraals! That's it, Cleve! Gray Rocks could have been the battleground."

"We have to go. There might be wounded and dying owls there that need help."

"There might be fighting owls there, as well," Otulissa said, and looked at Cleve, wishing for the umpteenth time that he had worn battle claws. "We have to approach carefully. Remember, there is not much cover."

But there was no need to approach carefully. A quarter of a league inland they began to sense an eerie stillness that was not the absence of the sounds of the Everwinter Sea and its crashing waves and grinding ice floes. This was the silence of death. They spotted the first body, that of a kraal, gilded, and glittering in the rising sun of the dawn, then a few yards away that of a pink-dyed kraal. As if to underscore the evidence they had found in the swirling eddy, there were a few unpainted feathers that spun through the air on that inexorable course to the coast. Something flinched in Otulissa's gizzard. If these were gadfeather owls, why? Kraals stole. Yes, they could get into trouble. But why gadfeathers? Gadfeathers were harmless. They lived only to sing.

"There's someone alive down there!" Cleve suddenly said. He swept down. "Great Glaux! It's Isa!"

They found a bloody mound of creamy feathers but Otulissa could tell immediately from the billowing of the chest plumage that the owl was still breathing.

"Isa, it's me, Cleve. What happened? Was it kraals?"

She gasped and then struggled for breath. "No, the kraals already dead. We just came to sing and . . . and . . ."

"And what?"

"Blue owls . . . with . . . with eggs." Cleve and Otulissa looked at each other.

"The eggs are here?" Otulissa asked urgently.

Cleve touched Otulissa with his wing. "Easy," he said.

"No, not here. Bad ice for schneddenfyrrs . . . to . . . to . . . to . . ." Cleve and Otulissa leaned closer. But there was only the sound of the Snowy's last breath, and then nothing.

"She was about to tell us where they took the eggs and then she . . ." Cleve's broad shoulders sagged. "I . . . I . . . can't believe she's gone. Her voice . . . She had the most beautiful voice in the Northern Kingdoms."

Otulissa extended her wing tip and touched Cleve softly. "I am sorry, Cleve. I am so sorry." Cleve straightened up and took a step toward Otulissa, spread his wings, and wrapped them around her. "This is terrible, Otulissa, terrible. And now we'll never know where the eggs are."

Otulissa stepped back. "No, Cleve, there is only one place they could take them that is hidden and where the ice is good quality for schneddenfyrrs." Cleve blinked. "The Ice Cliff Palace," Otulissa said. "That is the only place they could go."

"We should tell the others. Nut Beam can take the message."

"Not yet," Otulissa said. "We need more information. I want to know how many blue owls are involved in this. Did some leave in advance before . . . before this . . . this massacre?" She looked around at the slain owls. There were two dozen. How many had it taken to wreak this devastation? The kraals and gadfeathers had clearly been outnumbered.

Meanwhile, in his hollow at the great tree, Coryn blinked into the fire of his grate. It seemed he had been studying the flames for hours. He had sensed shapes, albeit vague ones, but he had a feeling that Tengshu's mission in the Middle Kingdom, his interview with the

H'ryth, was not going in the direction they had hoped. And he had sensed something else in the flames, in the way they licked up against each other's flanks. Coryn blinked several times and flicked his thin third eyelids to soothe his eyes and clear them of the fine ash kicked up from the grate. Then he peered again into the flames. It was as if pressure was building in the very gases of the fire. In a bulging flame, he caught an image with that unmistakable flicker of orange and a lick of blue at its center tinged with green: The ember. It began to tremble violently. Sparks seemed to fly from it. It was so real Coryn stepped back. "But it's just an image . . . just an image," Coryn whispered. The meaning, however, was clear. He could read the flames now. He saw a massing of not just owls but all sorts of creatures — wolves, bears, puffins, and others he could not make out. Then, like Tengshu, he realized that it was not a mere battle approaching but a war, the War of the Ember!

He knew immediately what he must do. Otulissa and Cleve were already in the Northern Kingdoms seeking out information about Nyra, the Striga, and whatever nefarious machinations they were up to. It was a spy mission, essentially. But Coryn knew now that the Guardians needed more than just information. They needed the help of every good creature they could muster for this war. *Who was left at the great tree who was not only seasoned in battle but extremely clever?* he thought.

"Kalo!" *Could she do it?* he wondered. Of course she could! Captured by the forces of the Striga, she had been condemned to death by fire. But there in the Shadow Forest, Coryn had found her and together they had confronted and fought her captors to the death. She was an owl of extraordinary courage, as was her younger brother, Cory. But despite their superior skills, Coryn felt he needed an owl whose experience went beyond courage. One whose knowledge of Nyra stretched far back. The answer was simple: Gwyndor. The Masked Owl had known Coryn from his very first days as a young hatchling in the canyonlands. He summoned the page who perched on the branch outside his hollow and asked him to fetch Gwyndor, Kalo, and Kalo's brother, Cory.

Coryn had met Kalo years before in the desert when he had been an outcast who was reviled by every owl in the kingdoms, because he so closely resembled his mother that he was often mistaken for her. But Kalo had befriended him and, in fact, he had saved the egg that would hatch to be her baby brother, whom they named Coryn in his honor. Kalo, young Coryn — or Cory as he was called — and Kalo's mate, Grom, now all lived at the tree.

Coryn reflected on the owls who would accompany him on this mission. Clever, diplomatic — that was essential — and strong. When they arrived in the hollow, he wasted no time. "Would you, Kalo, Gwyndor, and Cory, go with me to the Northern Kingdoms?"

Just then Octavia slithered in with some milkberry tea. Coryn blinked. *Odd time for tea,* he thought.

"Yes," Octavia said quietly. "I sense your surprise. But you know us nest-maid snakes. I sensed that you were agitated, Coryn. And now I have a feeling you are going to the Northern Kingdoms." Before Coryn could reply to Octavia, Kalo answered his question.

"The Northern Kingdoms!" Kalo exclaimed. "Oh, I have always wanted to go!"

"I don't suppose you might consider taking an old Northern Kingdom creature along?" Octavia interjected. "I do know the lay of the land, so to speak. And unlike the other nest-maid snakes I was not always blind."

"You weren't, Octavia?" Kalo asked.

"Oh no, my dear." She paused.

Gwyndor broke in. "Octavia flew with the original stealth unit of the Kielian League. She and Ezylryb."

"Great Glaux!" Kalo's beak dropped open in surprise.

"I know what you're going to say, Coryn — that was ancient history. Well, it was. We live long, we Kielian snakes. I flew with Ezylryb in the War of the Ice Claws — double wing commander and tail launcher in the Glauxspeed Division."

Kalo was in awe. "Glauxspeed Division! That was legendary."

"Didn't seem much like a legend or a fairy tale when I was flying tail, believe me!"

"What did you launch?" Kalo's brother Cory asked.

"Ice rockets. Can't be blind to do that. Quite a team we were back then. But we were both wounded. I, actually, the worst. Lost my eyes. So we hung up the battle claws — literally — and, well, to make a long story short, we sought a more quiet, scholarly life. We went to the Glauxian Brothers' retreat and eventually came here."

"But Octavia," Coryn said, "do you really want to go back there? I think bad times are coming."

"Yes, I sensed that. Your gizzard's in quite a turmoil. Mrs. P. sensed it, too."

"But you haven't done anything like this for years," Coryn said. The anxiety in his voice was clear. "And frankly, we'll need to move fast. This is no holiday jaunt."

Gwyndor felt a wince in his gizzard. No owl or snake liked being reminded of its age. He sympathized with

Octavia. She had a depth of knowledge about the Northern Kingdoms that none of them possessed.

"Look, Coryn." Octavia wound herself into a plump coil. "I know I am old. I know I can't fight the way I used to. But I know the Northern Kingdoms. Hoke of Hock is a distant cousin of mine. We go back. I know a lot of the owls in the Frost Beaks division and, of course, the old Glauxspeed. Not to mention that I speak fluent Krakish. Look, I know I'm fat. But I'll go on a diet immediately."

"You're not too fat for me to carry!" Kalo said enthusiastically. "You know how strong we Burrowing Owls are. And there are four of us. We can trade off."

"I can carry you, too, Octavia. I insist on doing my share," Cory quickly said.

Coryn didn't reply immediately. Cory was young, but bold and energetic. He rose to challenges. He had proved this already on two different occasions when he was determined to find and rescue his sister. "All right. You can come, Octavia." He paused and looked into the empty sockets of her eyes. "You are valuable. I should never underestimate your knowledge of the Northern Kingdoms and its creatures."

Had she not been eyeless, the old nest-maid would have shed tears. *This,* she thought, *is not just a noble king, but an owl with a generous gizzard.*

Plans were made for an immediate departure. Had Coryn cast one last glance at his fire he would have seen something of interest. The images flared in small tongues, looking owlish with roundish heads and the radiating facial feather patterns of Great Grays.

"Sir!" It was the page who interrupted Coryn just as he was about to look into the fire.

"Yes, what is it?"

"A coded message from Silver." The page handed him a piece of paper.

Coryn unfolded it and quickly translated. The ember had been retrieved from the palace. The three owls, numbers one, two, three, were progressing on their separate routes. So far, no enemy owls had been sighted in or around the palace. Estimates of distance covered was halfway for owl number one. *That's Ruby,* Coryn thought. Owl number two, one quarter way. *Wensel.* And owl number three, one-third of the way. *Fritha.*

Coryn crumpled up the note and put it in the grate. The message was purposely vague, but in fact there was very little that could be ascertained at this stage. At least the ember had been retrieved. *Now if only it could simply vanish forever!* Coryn thought. *My life will never be normal until the ties that bind me to this ember are broken. But what force shall break them?*

CHAPTER SEVENTEEN

# A Surprise Warrior

*Somewhere,* Otulissa was thinking as she and Cleve streamed through the canyon that split the cliffs of the Ice Talons, *somewhere behind the walls of ice and the looming spires that crowned them, there are clutches of fiendish eggs, pulsing inwardly with life. Perish the thought!* Had the murderous owls successfully transported their heinous treasure? Whoever was tending the eggs — most likely Nyra and the Striga — would need to remain concealed. She and Cleve were now looking for evidence, any clue of their whereabouts. A telltale blue feather. Anything. They had had ample time to get to the Ice Cliffs and tuck themselves into the maze of cracks and channeling fissures that penetrated deep into the cliffs and then opened into larger spaces perfect for schneddenfyrrs. *Perfect for infant hagsfiends.* Otulissa almost gagged at the thought. To use the words "infant" and "hagsfiend" in the same breath seemed perverted.

Otulissa's worst fears — that there was more than

one blue owl from the Middle Kingdom — had been confirmed. There was, indeed, a gang. Somehow they had been recruited from the Dragon Court. Why should it surprise her? If the Striga could strip himself of the cumbersome train of luxuriant feathers, why couldn't other dragon owls do so, as well? The Striga was a compelling, charismatic bird. He had rallied plenty of disaffected owls in the Hoolian world to his cause. It was not impossible that he could do the same in the Panqua Palace. Otulissa would put nothing past him.

Suddenly, a sapphire radiance suffused the glistening white walls of the ice canyon. "Duck!" Cleve hissed and both he and Otulissa plunged toward the surface of the ribbon of green water that furrowed in from the Everwinter Sea. Otulissa flipped her head up. Four enormous owls in a spectrum of colors ranging from cobalt to sapphire to azure and midnight blue flying above them had fixed them in their pale yellow gaze. *They're higher than we are! They have the advantage of altitude!* was Otulissa's first thought. But a quick assessment showed that they were not wearing battle claws. Still, they were fierce, trim, and ready to fight. And yet the owls were not chasing Otulissa or Cleve. They were not diving down after them, but rather making a phalanx above, closing off the free air, the sky, blocking any escape route except if the two Guardians flew straight out the end of this narrow corridor of ice. But the corridor twisted and turned. *It might grow even narrower, and the enemy might . . .* Otulissa did not want to think in terms of "might." She had to think of "now." But who knew what awaited them at the other end of the canyon? More dragon owls? They had flown into a section that was now too narrow in which to turn around and head back the way they had flown in. But why weren't the owls descending on them? This ran contrary to the most basic battle strategies. Otulissa had unlocked her own battle claws. These were the new models — the double-hinged retractables, sometimes referred to as "gizzard shredders."

"This is when it would help to be a puffin," Cleve muttered, thinking how they could swim underwater.

*It would help,* Otulissa thought, *if you wore battle claws!* But Cleve was a gizzard-resister. He did not believe in fighting. *Idiot!*

"Otulissa, look, the lower we go, the higher they go. Keep doing that!"

"Doing what?" She was truly irritated with Cleve for being unarmed.

"That thing with your tail." He and Otulissa were now skimming the water so closely that their undertail coverts were dragging and casting up a plume of spray. "They don't want to come down here, Otulissa. They're scared."

"Of what? Your battle claws?" Otulissa asked acidly.

"No, of the water, Otulissa! They don't want to get near the water!"

It was beginning to dawn on Otulissa. They were like hagsfiends, who had an instinctive terror of salt water. Then it seemed for a second as if all the air was being sucked out of the canyon. Otulissa felt herself stagger in flight, but she saw Cleve rocket straight up. *It's snowing,* Otulissa thought. *It's snowing blue feathers!*

## CHAPTER EIGHTEEN

# A Distracted Owl

Buried in a double layer of striated clouds that were streaming with ice crystals, Soren could still hear Wensel's passage through the air more than two hundred feet below. No owl could hear like a Barn Owl. "That frinking owl is getting distracted!" Soren fumed to Gylfie, who flew just beneath his port wing.

"Are you sure?" Although as soon as the words were out, she knew the question was ridiculous. After all these years she should know better than to question anything Soren might have heard.

"An artist!" Soren muttered.

"Too much imagination," Gylfie replied.

Creative, sensitive, and bold, Wensel was nevertheless off the flight plan by at least a quarter of a league. Soren didn't have to see it to know that Wensel had drifted in a southeasterly direction. It was almost as if Soren could hear the unspoken thoughts that were batting about in that artistic brain and making his gizzard flinch. *He's wondering, no doubt, if he is the one with the ember.* Soren sighed. The clouds were thinning in the lower stratum of the double layer. He could fly out of them to give Wensel a good cuff and remind him to get back to business.

And, truly, Wensel was wondering just that. *Do I carry the ember in this botkin? Could I tell if I looked down into the dozen or so coals? Would that lick of blue somehow be bluer than the other bonks? Would I see that wonderful indefinable green that I tried to paint in those legend illustrations and could never quite get? Does that green shine in my botkin?*

As Wensel's mind wandered so did his flight. Gylfie could tell Soren was getting more and more agitated. "I can hear that scraping sound off his wings, Gylf."

"What does that mean?"

"It means that Wensel is approaching the Great Horns."

"Oh, Glaux!" Gylfie exclaimed. "Old home week," she said sarcastically.

The two stony peaks that rose like the tufts of a Great Horned Owl in the canyonlands had, at one time, marked the entrance to St. Aegolius Academy for Orphaned Owls, where Soren and Gylfie had once been imprisoned. It had also been the site of a major confrontation in the War of Fire and Ice. A bad place to be. Easy to get trapped between the two horns. *Been there, done that.* And just at that moment Soren's gizzard lurched. He heard wing beats, new wing beats, not those of a Barn Owl. Messy, sloppy wing beats. And the whistling of air against featherless legs. More than just two legs, six at least. Which meant three owls.

"Gylfie," he hissed. "We've got visitors! Or rather Wensel does. Burrowing Owls!" Soren had known that sound at once; the scratch of the wind wrapping around the bare sinewy legs of Burrowing Owls. And Digger wasn't among these sloppy fliers. Digger had learned how to fly better than any Burrowing Owl he had ever encountered. These three owls, Soren could tell, were definitely tracking Wensel. The contingency plan in such an event was to go to ground if the pursued owl could not lose the pursuers. But going to ground with Burrowing Owls was the last thing one would want to do. They were excellent on the ground. They could run, dig, even heave rocks with those long legs. Wensel wouldn't have a chance.

But Wensel was not a Barn Owl for nothing. He could hear as well as any other and suddenly the sickening sound of that wind against bare legs pierced his musings. *Holy racdrops! I'm being followed.* In that same instant, the lower-level clouds peeled back. Threads of lightning tormented the sky and illuminated the two Great Horns. In another few seconds, he would be trapped between them. He glanced back at his pursuers. His gizzard gave a painful twist. They were wearing battle claws, and not just any battle claws, but fire claws. The tip of each claw glowed with the embedded coals. Wensel felt himself begin to lose altitude. His wings had locked. *I am dropping. I am going yeep.*

*Frinkin' racdrops!* Soren thought. "Extend!" he called to Gylfie.

There were three clicks. One click as the single-action prongs of Soren's battle claws extended and two more as the double hinges of Gylfie's unlocked.

# CHAPTER NINETEEN
# *High Stakes*

Amazing!" Otulissa said. She was bobbling around on a chunk of ice that had been dislodged from the canyon wall when Cleve had performed the most basic and powerful of all Danyar moves, the Breath of Qui. A student of the Danyar, the way of noble gentleness, never used weapons that butchered an enemy. Instead, Danyar focused on developing the entire owl organism — its joints, its hollow bones, its gizzard, lungs, heart, and feathers — so that an owl could strike with great force using every part and fiber of its body. The Breath of Qui was a massive inhalation that expanded an owl's lungs to four times their normal size. It was this inhalation and exhalation that were the central elements in the Danyar style of fighting. It most certainly did kill, but in a way that is what the Jouzhen owls call "owlyk," which meant as bloodlessly and painlessly as possible.

Cleve had just performed the Breath of Qui and now

the bodies of four owls were rapidly sinking into the sea. They were dead by the time they had hit the surface of the water, but what was intriguing was how their feathers had become instantly sodden. They might as well have been stones. Otulissa blinked several times. She was not sure what astonished her more, Cleve performing the Breath of Qui and felling the owls with one exhalation or the fact that the blue owls were already nearly swallowed by the sea. She blinked again and looked up at Cleve. She felt absolutely foolish wearing her double-hinged retractable battle claws with their single-action recoil — *whatever, blah, blah, blah,* she thought. *So much for technology.* He had dispatched the blue owls bare-clawed!

Otulissa tried to compose herself. "Cleve," she gasped, "I know how you did it, but how and when did you learn?" But before the question was answered, she remembered Dumpy asking Cleve on the flight here why he and Tengshu had exchanged that funny look just before Tengshu left for the Middle Kingdom. "Funny?" Cleve had asked somewhat disingenuously. "Maybe it was just a nervous tic." It came back to Otulissa now. She stood up straighter on the bobbling ice block. "You told Dumpy you had a nervous tic. But you don't have any such thing, do you, Cleve?"

"No, my dear, none whatsoever. It would have been difficult for me to learn the way of noble gentleness if I had had a nervous tic."

"So you've been studying with Tengshu?"

Cleve nodded.

"Behind my back?" Otulissa's voice almost broke as she spoke the words.

"Oh, Otulissa, I feared I might fail. I have never in my life fought before. I am not a fighting owl."

"But why now? Why did you decide to learn?"

"I had forebodings. When I came to the tree and heard about the Striga and all that he had done and that he had not been killed — I just felt . . . I don't know. I think it was love more than fear. I want to do all I can to protect you, and what you value. The tree."

"So you took up arms for me?" Otulissa asked incredulously.

"Not arms. I learned the way of Danyar. I think things are going to be bad, Otulissa. I think a big war is coming, what with the Striga and Nyra trying to bring the hagsfiends back to life for this war. The stakes are so high. The ember and . . . *you.*"

## CHAPTER TWENTY

# Standoff at the Great Horns

Soren blinked. He could not believe that he and Gylfie were in a standoff. Somehow, Wensel had shaken off his fear, regained flight, and unlocked his wings before crashing, but now Soren, Gylfie, and Wensel were perched directly under the twin shadows of the Great Horns, opposite the three Burrowing Owls who were advancing on them, the burning tips of their fire claws glaring like eyeballs from hagsmire. Soren was incredulous. They were only just past half-way to the Wolf's Fang. They probably would have been there by now if Wensel hadn't wandered off route. Did Wensel have the ember? Soren hoped he didn't. He wished with all his gizzard that Ruby or Fritha had it, and were already at the Wolf's Fang. Nonetheless, this was a dangerous situation. The numbers on each side were even, but their sizes were not. Burrowing Owls were larger than Barn Owls, and about four times the size of Gylfie.

"What'cha got in that botkin, lad?" It was Tarn who spoke. Soren recognized him. Tarn, architect and chief excavator of the extensive burrowing encampment that the Pure Ones had set up in the Desert of Kuneer before the battle in the Middle Kingdom. He had been the highest-ranking officer below Nyra in the Pure Ones. *Who is he working for now?* Soren wondered. But then a voice out of nowhere cawed.

"Hey, he ain't blue," said the unexpected voice from high up on one of the Great Horns.

"And that other one ain't no Barn Owl," cracked another.

The six owls on the ground all looked up, startled, to see where these voices came from. Soren jerked his head back. He had to strike now while Tarn and the other two Burrowing Owls were distracted. He hurled himself into flight while the others were still looking up.

"You go, owl!" the voice from above them hooted. *This is incredible,* Soren thought. He caught a flash of silver streaking down from the peaks of the Great Horns as he struck at the Burrowing Owl nearest to him and sent him tumbling. *Gotta get him into the air!* Soren thought. In the air above, swirling around the peaks, there were more flashes of silvery gray from which taunts began raining down.

*He ain't blue and he ain't Barn,*
*Holy racdrops, it must be Tarn!*
*They say he be a genius owl.*
*Say he's a genius, I say he's a dud,*
*Bad-butt owl just like old Kludd!*

Was it Twilight? Two Twilights? The Great Grays were everywhere all at once — and Wensel! Wensel had just taken a piece of brush and, in an insanely daring move, flown directly at Tarn, igniting the brush from his opponent's fire claws. *Now that's inventive! And crazy!* Soren thought. *But who are these Grays?* The odds had definitely improved with the intervention of the Grays, and Wensel had lit another branch and passed it off to the larger of the two. Gylfie had dashed in and caught a twig midair that had dropped from one of the burning branches. Gylfie could be positively lethal with a burning twig.

*Let it burn, let it burn!*
*Oh, let it burn, burn him not you!*
*A nice burrow stew!*
*Burn their butts naked as their legs,*
*Now just watch them start to beg.*

"Hey, Cletus!" the other Great Gray shouted. "Got me a stick — it's all on fire." In a daring sweep, he rushed in, skimming, just out of reach of the enemy owl's fire claws, and knocked him off balance. As the owl staggered, Gylfie darted in and ignited his tail feathers with her twig in an almost balletic movement.

In another two seconds, the owl was consumed in flames. This was all the other two Burrowing Owls needed to see, and they were off in a flash, streaking through the night with the fire claws that had been their undoing.

Soren, Gylfie, and Wensel collapsed, exhausted. "It's all my fault!" Wensel said.

"You're right about that," Soren said wearily. "But you sure fought well and you never lost the grip on the botkin." Soren then turned to the two Great Grays.

"Who are you?"

"Cletus," said the smaller of the two.

"Cletus? That's your name?"

"Nobody else's." He turned to the other owl. "Brother Tavis, you know anyone else called Cletus?"

"Can't say as I do, brother."

"Don't tell me you're from the orphan school of tough learning?"

The one called Tavis shook his head. "No . . . no, not really. We were pretty well raised until . . ." His voice dwindled off.

"Until when?"

"Until the night Cletus and I went out hunting for our mum. You see, she was sitting an egg. It was supposed to hatch soon. Our da had already died. Killed by one of the earliest leaders of the Pure Ones."

"Long before Metal Beak," Cletus added. "You've heard of Metal Beak?"

Soren nodded.

"Well," Tavis continued, "when we came back she was gone. It looked as if the egg had hatched."

"We didn't know what happened." Cletus now picked up the story. "Then a few nights later we found her body. But no signs of a chick. Just gone. Probably killed."

Tavis stepped forward and spoke now. "The times were really bad. There were St. Aggie's raids going on all over the place. We were young so we just decided to go underground."

"Literally!" Cletus interjected.

"Yeah, we went to the Desert of Kuneer and lived for a long time in abandoned burrows."

"That's why we could fight these suckers so well. We know the ways of Burrowing Owls. And yeah, we've heard of this Tarn. Bad-butt owl!"

"But we always wondered what happened to the chick, our brother or sister. Don't even know which," Tavis said in a voice that seemed to ache with sorrow.

Soren and Gylfie looked at each other in quiet astonishment. The similarities were not just remarkable but extraordinary — the brashness, the humor, the nonstop beak! And, of course, the spot-on fighting skills — all obviously learned in the infamous orphan school of tough learning to which their dear friend Twilight was constantly referring.

"I think I know what happened to that owlet," Soren said softly.

"You know?" The two Great Grays were stunned.

"He lives."

"He lives!" the two owls cried joyously, and seemed to swell like smoky moons in the wind-torn night.

CHAPTER TWENTY-ONE

# A Mustering of Troops

It was like a current, a current not of wind or of water, but of apprehension and then resolve that swept through the Northern Kingdoms. A polar bear was doing something she had never done before as she plunged into the choppy water, leaving the den she had just cleaned out and fixed for winter. She began swimming out the Bay of Kiel and her usual winter territory in an easterly direction toward the Firth of Fangs, where Svarr, father of her cubs, resided for the winter. The ice was getting thicker as she swam north. She used her hind paws to steer herself around ice floes, which were becoming more numerous. Soon an entire ice field materialized. It was the outer apron of the H'rathghar glacier, a very good seal-hunting ground, and as Sveep turned her boulder-sized head, she caught sight of a tendril of vapor winding up from a hole. Undoubtedly a seal breathing hole. Normally, she would have stopped, hoisted herself out of the water, waited for the seal to poke its snout out of the hole, and then, springing, she would have grabbed its head in her immense serrated fangs and had herself a nice snack. But she didn't have time. She had to get up the firth.

"Grischtung issen micht micht." She muttered the ancient Krakish oath, an oath of wonder and dismay as she swam. It was indeed a wonder that the young puffin had done what she had said he should. The tubby, awkward bird had actually flown to the great tree and, now, unbelievably, a king had come to visit her. Coryn, the three owls with him, and an ancient Kielian snake had arrived on the edges of an early winter storm. It seemed that what the puffin, Dumpy — was that his name? Yes — what Dumpy had witnessed in the cave in the Ice Narrows had much more serious implications than she had thought. Coryn was surprised but infinitely grateful that Sveep had traveled the overland trail to speak with Gyllbane. He had not known about the moon cycles Gyllbane spent with Sveep in her summer den after Cody's death.

"After your long journey," Coryn had said hesitantly as he peered into the immense dark pools of Sveep's eyes, "I feel that I don't have the right to ask another favor of you. But a war is coming and it will not be just a war between owls. It will touch every place and every creature in the Southern and the Northern kingdoms. So we need the help of all creatures — be they owls, wolves, or bears. We have to fight for the freedom, the dignity of all animals. If this war comes it will not be won by evacuation, nor will it be won by animals hunkering down in their burrows or their winter dens until the fighting ends. We need to muster an expeditionary force. Sveep, you have done so much already. Do you think you can recruit and lead a fighting force of polar bears?"

The polar bear had agreed. Already she had gathered the non-pregnant females who denned near her to meet her at a designated time on the westernmost shore of the Bay of Kiel, where they would travel the overland route and find their way to Beyond the Beyond. Sveep was not sure why, but the king said that the Beyond would be the battleground. She was just approaching the inlet where Svarr denned and began emitting soft sonorous growls to greet him.

"Aaargh!" The reply came from deep in the den. She had been heard. Sveep rolled on her back, folded her huge paws across her stomach, and floated about while she waited for Svarr to come to the entrance of his cave. Finally, he appeared. He looked cross.

"What in the name of Ursa are you doing here?"

"A visit."

"It's not that time."

"I know. What do you think I am . . ." She was about to say "a stupid puffin?" but she clamped her mouth shut.

Sveep sighed and then said crisply, "Look, conversation closed about cubs and all that stuff."

"All that stuff! You're talking, madam, of my progeny." Svarr tried to look nobly offended, but only succeeded in looking crotchety.

"Don't look so crotchety." She knew this would get him.

"Old bears are crotchety. I'm not an old bear."

Sveep knew she had him just where she wanted him now. She'd injured his pride. Nothing like a war to make a male polar bear feel fit. She rolled over onto her stomach and paddled to the lip of the ice of his den and rested her elbows on it. She drew her face very close to his. "All right, big guy!" The pleasant odor of the bluescales that she had consumed on her swim north washed over Svarr's face as she spoke. "Now listen to me. This is the time for all brave bears to come together. Noble bears, bears of valor." She could see Svarr's eyes fasten on her. His surliness had dissolved. There was only the black intensity of his eyes. "I have been charged by a king, King Coryn from the great tree, to form a fighting division of polar bears."

"You?"

Sveep ignored his dismay. "Listen to me, Svarr. You are a bear of valor, an *ursus maritimus.* A bear of the sea and the land as well. In our world, it has been the noble Guardians of the Great Ga'Hoole Tree that have fought the good fight. We have lived apart in a world bound by ice and sea. But there has never been, in all of time, a chance like this for us polar bears. We can go forth now, to guard our land against a terrible threat from ancient times." She paused to let that sink in.

"What threat from ancient times?"

"Hagsfiends." She noted the shock in his dark eyes, like a little flinch in the darkness of a moonless night. "Listen to me, Svarr. We have in our sinew, our muscles, our paws, our sheer size, instruments for shattering power. We possess colossal strength. Now of whom else might this be said? Join me, Svarr. Swim with me and we shall fight the good fight and help the Guardians of the Great Ga'Hoole Tree win this war."

As Sveep swam out of the Firth of Fangs with her sometime mate following, high overhead, buried in the last of the stria clouds, Coryn, Gwyndor, Kalo, and her brother, Cory, flew up the firth to visit the old warrior Moss. They took turns carrying Octavia, who did seem to have grown sleeker on the arduous flight. Just before nearing Moss's territory Gwyndor took Octavia on his back and flew toward Stormfast Island for a parlay with Octavia's distant relative, Hoke of Hock.

Although infirmed and barely able to fly himself, Moss was still the commander in chief of all the armed owls of the Northern Kingdoms, which included the Frost Beaks, the Glauxspeed division, and an all-female unit of mostly Snowy Owls, many of them former gadfeathers who flew with the deadly ice scimitars. They were ironically known as the Sissies, which was short for Screaming Ice Scimitars. Coryn would ask Moss to provide troops for the war.

After Gwyndor's departure with Octavia on board, Coryn, Kalo, and Cory continued on course up the firth for some time in silence. Coryn was surprised when a Snowy and a Barred Owl flew out from the lagoon where Moss was said to nest. "We have been expecting you," they announced.

Coryn blinked in confusion.

"Nut Beam told us," the Snowy Owl said. "He wanted to get an urgent message to you. He had heard that you were flying this way. The message is from Otulissa, and Cleve. She says it is imperative that you fly to the Ice Dagger immediately."

Coryn swiveled his head toward Kalo and blinked. "I think you should go, Coryn," Kalo said. "We can convey your request to Moss."

The Barred Owl nodded his head in agreement. "I think Moss knows why you have come. Permit me, Coryn, to escort your companions to Moss. You should feel free to take your leave of us to meet with Otulissa and our old friend Cleve."

So Coryn turned back. At least the wind had shifted and would be behind him now. It was pretty much a straight shot to the Ice Dagger. *What has Otulissa found out now?* he wondered. Perhaps he could get back to the tree earlier than expected. Time was of the essence.

He didn't realize quite how essential it truly was.

In another part of the Northern Kingdoms on Stormfast Island, Octavia arranged herself in a coil and held her head erect it as she prepared to address Hoke of Hock. Gwyndor had dropped her on the barren island and made himself scarce to give the old compatriots some time alone. Like Octavia, Hoke was a glistening green-blue snake. He was not, however, blind.

"Octavia, old friend," he said. "It has been much too long."

"Yes, Hoke. Too many years."

"I understand that our dearest comrade Lyze, or Ezylryb as you called him in the Southern Kingdoms, has died."

Octavia nodded her head slowly.

"Now what brings you here?"

"War," Octavia said simply.

"I have heard no news of war. I only hear of good things about your king, the one who seized the ember."

"Yes, and he is good and he has the ember in his power — for now."

A quiver went through Hoke's long slender body. He was draped over a pinnacle of ice that jutted out nearly perpendicular from the rock. "For now? Explain! Tell me!"

And so Octavia began to plead eloquently, hoping that Hoke would agree to support the guardians with a squadron of Kielian snakes. "Hoke, you trained the original stealth force of Kielian snakes. It was Lyze who recruited you for the War of the Ice Claws. And now I ask you in the name of Lyze and all the values that noble owl embodied, join us."

"I am surely too old," Hoke replied.

"Your body is old but not your mind."

Hoke wound himself tighter around the ice pinnacle. "Rest assured. You will have all that you need. The elite force commanded by my grandson, Harlo, will be dispatched to the Southern Kingdoms. And you say the king has gone to seek out Moss?"

Octavia nodded.

Hoke slithered down the pinnacle and settled himself on a rock surface. "It's interesting. I saw a polar bear who frequents this area making her way northward, north and west as if she was going up the Firth of Fangs. Odd time of year to see polar bears out and about. However, I don't suppose the polar bears know yet of this business."

"Oh, but they do!" Octavia exclaimed. "A puffin informed them. It was actually a puffin who came and told us about Nyra and the Striga in the Ice Narrows."

"A puffin!" Hoke hissed in amazement.

"Yes, our reaction as well, but apparently this one is somewhat brighter."

"An intelligent puffin!" Hoke waggled his head slowly in a wonder. "That would be a sight to see!"

At the very moment Hoke was marveling over the rumored intelligence of Dumpy, forty puffins perched on the ridge where puffins of the Ice Narrows lived. "Something big is coming," Dumpy addressed them. "I mean, really big." Dumpy's eyes widened as he tried to convey the bigness, the seriousness of what he was going to explain.

"How big? Big as your butt?" one puffin shouted.

"Knock it off," said another puffin.

"It was a joke," said the first.

"Well, it's not funny, so knock it off." At which point the jokester raised a webbed foot, smacked herself in the head, and succeeded in knocking herself off the ledge into the churning waters. There was a swell of raucous puffin laughter. Dumpy blinked, then shut his eyes for several seconds. This was going to be difficult. He had to figure out a way to catch these birds' ever-wandering attention.

Dumpy opened his eyes slowly and spoke carefully and distinctly, but in a low voice so they had to lean forward to hear him. "If you be quiet and listen, I will tell you a very big secret."

"What's that? What's that?" They pressed close to him, looking eager and alert.

"The secret is that I have been to the Great Ga'Hoole Tree."

"Oooh," they all sighed.

"I have spoken to their king."

There were more oohs.

"I have spoken to the king's counselors."

"What's a counselor?" someone whispered.

"An ornament," another said.

Dumpy forged ahead. "And the secret that I have to tell you is that we are not nearly so dumb as we have always thought. Indeed, we each have a brain."

"We do?" It was the Chubster who spoke now. "Are you sure, Dumpy?"

"Yes, I am sure. And if you use it, it gets better and better, and you get smarter and smarter. And I am going to show you how to use it. Now what do we know best in all the world?"

"Fish," said a tiny little female named Popo.

"Right you are. See, Popo used her brain. And what do we do most?' "

"Fish," said another puffin.

"And what happens when we leave a fish out for a long time without our eating it?" Dumpy asked.

"It freezes stiff and you can almost break your beak on it."

"Mummy says no playing with frozen fish. They're dangerous," Popo piped up.

"Exactly, Popo." Dumpy paused. "Dangerous like swords. Like daggers! They could even be weapons."

"Weapons!" they exclaimed. They all knew somewhat dimly about weapons. Some of them had seen owls fly through the Ice Narrows with their battle claws gleaming.

"Yes," Dumpy went on, "and the big thing I was trying to tell you about — the big thing that is coming is bad owls. The Guardians of the great tree are going to fight the bad owls and they need all the help they can get. We are going to help them."

"But Dumpy, aren't we just too darned dumb?" the Chubster said.

"No!" Dumpy exploded. "There will be no more D word!"

"D word?" they all said, for not one of them had any notion of letters, their sounds, or what they might signify.

"No more saying the word 'dumb,'" Dumpy explained. "You are going to become fighting puffins. Fighting the good fight for the noble owls of the Great Ga'Hoole Tree. We can do it. But you must believe that you can think. To fish is to be a puffin. To build an ice hollow is to be a puffin, but to think is also to be a puffin."

And thus it was that the Dump Brigade began, not just named for its leader Dumpy the Fifteenth, but for three out of four of the puffins, as well, who made up that first brigade and who were also named Dumpy. And their first exercise was target practice with frozen fish. They soon found that the tiny slim capelin were easier to launch and more precise in their trajectory than the rather cumbersome bluescales. Yes, "trajectory." The puffins did start to speak in such terms as trajectory, velocity, and the speed of the airflow around frozen capelins, bluescales, and herring hurled at distant targets.

# CHAPTER TWENTY-TWO

# A Summit Meeting

"We think that their target date for this . . . this vile hatching is the night of the lunar eclipse," said Otulissa. With Cleve at her side, she was perched on the Ice Dagger, which jutted out from the depths of the Everwinter Sea. She and Cleve were telling Coryn what they'd learned in the Ice Narrows.

Coryn felt his gizzard quake. Owls had been talking forever about the peculiarities of young chicks who hatched on the night of a lunar eclipse. He himself had been born on such a night, as had his mother, and as had Hoole. In the back of his mind, a vague notion had been stirring. It was becoming clearer as Otulissa and Cleve related to him their discovery of the remnants of a strange egg in the Ice Narrows, and the horrible massacre at the Gray Rocks, and finally the alarming encounter with blue owls in the canyon of the Ice Talons. In an all-out war the Guardians might succeed in destroying the eggs and preventing the reentry of nachtmagen into the world. But the problem of the ember would remain and the ember itself, with its strange unfathomable powers, seemed to attract its own kind of poison from the world and the creatures in it.

Even though he was deep in thought, Coryn followed what Otulissa was saying. "We have until the eclipse. We don't know exactly where the eggs are but we have a pretty good idea. Cleve and I feel that if Nyra and the Striga could be lured away, even temporarily, we could destroy the eggs. We are sure more blue owls are being brought in to guard them but they are not there yet. I spoke to you about how we had encountered some kraals and they were an invaluable source of information on this. Cleve has learned much in his practice with Tengshu. I think he and I could handle whoever might be sent in to sit the eggs."

Coryn felt a stirring deep in his gizzard. It was almost as if he could feel glints deep within it and then there dawned a sudden brightness in his head, an illumination in his brain. "Well, of course!"

"Of course what?"

"The way to get them away — 'lure' them as you say — is with the ember."

"But aren't we trying to get the ember to the Middle Kingdom? Hide the ember? Not put it out there as bait!" Otulissa was astonished by Coryn's line of thinking.

"Otulissa." Coryn looked at her steadily then swung his head toward Cleve. "The ember is the only way! Believe me. It is our only chance for getting at those eggs. Besides, I am far from certain that Gup Theosang will give permission to hide the ember in his kingdom. While we wait for word, it will serve as bait."

"He's right, Otulissa," Cleve said.

"But how do we do it?"

"We will start with rumors of the ember."

"Rumors of it where?" Otulissa asked. There was doubt in her voice.

"In the Beyond. That's where it came from . . ." Coryn broke off speaking. He had started to say, "And that is where it belongs," but he stopped.

"It's very risky, I think," Otulissa began, "using the ember this way . . . but . . . but . . ."

"Hagsfiends are risky," Coryn said. "Nachtmagen is risky. It must be done," Coryn said resolutely.

"Are you sure, Coryn?" Otulissa pressed. "You are risking everything."

"But what will any of us have in a world with hagsfiends flying about?"

He turned now to Cleve. He did not want to argue

this point any longer. "You said that after you discovered the massacre at the Gray Rocks and your engagement with the blue owls in the Ice Narrows, you came across some kraals?"

"Yes, and gadfeathers. They had witnessed the carnage left by the massacre, and helped the few survivors get away. Needless to say, they are furious — and ready to fight."

Coryn's dark eyes glittered. "Could the two of you fly back to the great tree? Tell Madame Plonk that I would like her to fly to the Northern Kingdoms, to the places where the gadfeathers gather. See if she could muster a company of gadfeather owls, and kraals as well."

"I don't know if the gadfeathers can fight, Coryn," Otulissa said. "I mean, they have no experience. They sing."

"They are angry, Otulissa. Their own kind have been slaughtered. Don't underestimate passion. The passion they put into their songs can be put into combat. And anybody from the Northern Kingdoms can handle a short blade.

"So," Coryn continued. "Not only must you tell Madame Plonk to seek the help of the gadfeathers, but I have a special mission for Doc Finebeak."

"Crows? You want him to recruit crows?" Otulissa asked.

"Yes!" Doc Finebeak had enjoyed a long and productive relationship with the very birds that most owls feared. Crows. He was revered by crows. "But more. I want him to go to Ambala."

Coryn did not even need to finish the sentence. Otulissa knew exactly what he intended. If the Mysticus had instigated the turn in the Battle of the Book in the canyonlands the Greenowls of Ambala had turned the Battle of Balefire Night when the Striga and his followers had been driven from the tree with their help.

"And now, I must be off," Coryn said.

"But where are you going?" Otulissa asked.

"It's better that you not know for now, Otulissa."

"Really?" There was a plaintive note in her voice. Otulissa was as close to Coryn as any owl in the great tree except Soren. It was she who had found him alone, despondent, an outcast in the Beyond. It had been Otulissa, a master collier herself, who had started to teach the young owl the fine art of colliering at the Sacred Ring of volcanoes.

Coryn was a natural. She had never seen an owl so quick to learn. Otulissa had watched him retrieve the Ember of Hoole. Many had tried to retrieve the ember in the thousand years since Hoole had restored it to the volcanoes, but none had succeeded. Not until Coryn had come. Thus a special bond had been forged between the Spotted Owl and the young king. Otulissa had been as much of a confidante to Coryn as his uncle Soren.

Coryn now reached out with the tip of his port wing and touched her shoulder softly. "Don't worry, old friend. It's better you not know."

"Of course." Otulissa nodded. "Glaux speed, Coryn!" she murmured as she watched him spread his wings and lift off.

## CHAPTER TWENTY-THREE

# At the Wolf's Fang

One by one the owls had dropped out of the fast-scudding striated clouds into the mist that swirled around a rock that looked like a wolf's fang on the far western edge of the Sea of Vastness. But now the rock was almost completely obscured by fog. *Perfect Ezylryb weather,* Soren thought. But Soren did not need visual cues to find the Wolf's Fang. Tilting his head this way, then that, expanding and contracting his facial muscles to scoop up the finer nuances of the breaking waves as they encountered an obstacle in their course, he was able to triangulate the exact position of this rock entirely from sound clues. And, of course, he had Gylfie with him. The Elf Owl need not see the sun or the stars. The celestial charts were emblazoned on her brain. She could fly blindly through any weather and sense precisely how many points she was from, say, the port claw of the Little Raccoon constellation, on a night when most birds would be thoroughly confused. Soren, however, was relieved to know that the others had already arrived at the Wolf's Fang because he could hear the brush of the wind through their feathers.

He was full of hope now. Surely Tengshu would have gotten permission from the H'ryth for the passage of the ember. But uppermost in his mind at this moment before landing on the Wolf's Fang was how to tell Twilight the unbelievable news that he had two brothers who were very much alive. He had asked Tavis and Cletus not to accompany them to the Wolf's Fang, but rather to remain at the remote inlet where the Sea of Vastness furrowed in along a desolate stretch of the coastline. He needed to prepare Twilight for the meeting. But he was not sure how to do this. Tavis and Cletus had agreed to hang back but they were more than eager, indeed, almost feverish to meet their long-lost younger brother.

When Soren, Gylfie, and Wensel arrived, they were surprised to see not only Ruby, Martin, Fritha, and Digger, but Tengshu as well. Almost immediately, Soren sensed the despair that swirled as thickly as the fog around the rock.

"What is it?" he asked.

Tengshu shook his head slowly.

"You mean we can't take it there?"

Tengshu sighed. "Correct. Theosang will not accept the ember. And that is not all. There's another problem, Soren."

"It's awful," Martin muttered.

"What is it? Tell me!" Soren was almost hopping up and down. His gizzard twitched madly.

"There have been more defections from the Dragon Court," Tengshu said quietly.

"What?" Soren blinked. "What are you talking about?"

Tengshu quickly explained. Soren listened and nodded as each dreadful piece of information was revealed. He was beginning to learn what Otulissa, Cleve, and Coryn already knew. Finally, he spoke when Tengshu had finished. "So what you are telling me is that not only do we have no hope of sequestering this ember far away in a safe refuge in the Middle Kingdom, but by every indication these Dragon Court owls have been recruited by the Striga who has, as we know, joined forces with Nyra?"

The owls nodded.

Soren sighed. "What could be worse?"

And it was only seconds later that Primrose dropped out of the sky with a message clasped in her beak. "It's urgent," she said, giving it to Soren.

"It's in code. Gylfie, you're more fluent with the code than I am."

They unfurled the scroll and with Twilight anchoring one end and Digger the other, Gylfie hunched over the message.

"It's direct from Coryn. Well, the good news is that Coryn, for his own reasons, feels we should not under any circumstances take the ember to the Mountain of Time in the Middle Kingdom but . . ." She stopped translating abruptly.

"But what?" Twilight asked. Gylfie's eyes, normally bright sunny as a day, darkened. "There are hagsfiends aborning — it will happen on the night of the lunar eclipse. To stop it we must use the ember as a lure, so the eggs will be left unguarded and can then be destroyed."

"Of course!" Tengshu exclaimed. "That's why the Dragon Court owls are here." Tengshu paused. No one said a word. "You see, these Dragon Court owls are poor fighters, but they can be used for something much more dangerous."

"What's that?" Soren whispered.

"Broodies," Tengshu said hoarsely. "Broodies to hatch hagsfiends, to bring back nachtmagen. It was all there in the second section of the Theo Papers, called The Obscura. Perhaps not stated directly, for that is the nature of the writings in the 'Obscura.' Reading the material is similar to conversing with scrooms — - incomplete, many possible meanings. But there was an intimation that there could be a time when hagsfiends might return. Within the flabby gizzards of those Dragon Court owls are the seeds long dormant of . . . of . . . of . . ."

"Hagsfiends," Digger said. "The Dragon Court owls were, you think, in earlier generations the hagsfiends from the Kingdom of N'yrthghar, the ones we read about in the legends?"

"No one knows for sure," Tengshu replied.

"Theo did," Digger said.

"Perhaps," Tengshu replied quietly.

"He used the lure of the promise of everlasting power, splendor, and riches to lure them to the Dragon Court. And now we are to use the lure of the ember to prevent the rise of hagsfiends," Soren said.

"So it seems." Tengshu nodded.

"So it says, right here," Gylfie said, looking up from the coded message. "And there is one more thing. A slink melf is being dispatched by Coryn to the Ice Talons."

"A slink melf?" Twilight said. "You mean an assassination squadron?"

"Yes, to finish off the eggs."

"Who makes up the slink melf?" Twilight asked.

"The message doesn't say. It just says it's being ordered by Coryn. But it's obviously not us. We are to report to the volcanoes of the Sacred Ring immediately."

"All right, but we have to go by way of the inlet," Soren said.

"But that's out of the way, and what with this wind, it will slow us down," Gylfie protested.

"No, I insist. I think ultimately it will help our cause," Soren replied, thinking of the two Great Grays. Tavis and Cletus were incredibly cunning fliers, agile and quick just like their brother Twilight. The Guardians could use such help.

## CHAPTER TWENTY-FOUR

# An Old Friend

In a lava cave not far from the Sacred Ring of volcanoes, Coryn perched on a black outcropping and spoke to the first friend he had ever made in the desolate country known as Beyond the Beyond. Hamish, the once-lame gnaw wolf, had been listening attentively.

"So who composes this slink melf, Coryn?" Hamish asked. As all gnaw wolves of the MacDuncan clan, he had gone into training and become a member of the Watch at the Sacred Ring of volcanoes. When Coryn had retrieved the Ember of Hoole from H'rathghar, Hamish, as had been mystically prophesied in the time of Hoole, was cured of his lameness and allowed to return to normal life. Now these two old friends met again.

"I've just come from Gyllbane's clan cave. You must know what she learned from the polar bear."

Hamish nodded.

"So you know of the conspiracy between the Striga and Nyra."

He nodded again.

"The eggs I just told you about — that is the slink melf's mission: to destroy them and any owls that are brooding them."

"I certainly didn't know about the eggs, at least not what you are now telling me. Gyllbane, or rather, Namara, as she now should be called, is the best choice for the slink melf. And you say she is on her way?"

"Yes," Coryn replied.

Hamish looked at Coryn carefully. "But you seem to have something more on your mind."

Coryn sighed. He tipped his head down and studied his talons. He could not bring himself to say what he must say while looking into the green eyes of the gnaw wolf he had met on his very first night in the Beyond.

"Hamish, dear friend." He paused. "Dearest wolf friend. We know each other so well that sometimes words are not needed."

"Like now," Hamish said quietly.

"You know what I am about to ask."

"You want to return the ember to the volcanoes," Hamish said steadily.

Coryn raised his head and the two friends peered into the each other's eyes. In Hamish's eyes, Coryn saw that green light, the same green that flickered near the center of the ember. He blinked and closed his eyes tight. "And when I return the ember, you become lame again. I am asking you to give up all hope of a normal life. Of finding a mate or rearing young."

"You are also delivering the world from nachtmagen, Coryn," Hamish said quietly. "You forget, Coryn, that when you retrieved the ember, not only were our twisted limbs repaired but we were given a choice. And we all chose to remain as wolves so that we could continue to serve." The words of Fengo, the head gnaw wolf of the Sacred Watch, came back like a dim echo in his brain. *We have all chosen to remain as wolves, to serve you, King Coryn, but we have also chosen to regain what we had lost in order to serve the Sacred Ring. Our twisted limbs have been straightened. Our eyes restored, our tails made whole once more. But we shall always be prepared to serve you, good King Coryn, always. That is our pledge.*

"So, Hamish. You agree to this?"

"We all do, Coryn. We are the Watch."

"Tell no one yet. None of the Guardians know that I mean to return the ember, not even the Band. And

Hamish . . ." Coryn stopped and churred softly to himself.

"What is it?"

"I just had the oddest thought."

"What is that, Coryn?"

"I was thinking that if it were put to me what I would choose to be in my life, and I could be any creature, I would not choose to be an owl." He now peered down into the drip bowl in Hamish's cave, where water collected from the seeping cracks in the rock when it rained. He studied the reflection, with the scar that cut diagonally across his face. The mirror image of his mother's face gazed back at him. He tried to imagine his face without the scar, but the scar no longer bothered him. "If I could choose to be any other creature I would choose to be a wolf, Hamish."

"You would give up wings?"

Coryn shrugged. "I know. It doesn't make sense. I would be earthbound. I can't explain it. But yes, I would choose to be a wolf and give up wings."

*And right now, the future of the owl kingdom depends, in fact, on two wolves, Hamish and Namara,* Coryn thought. *And Glaux willing, she is nearly to the Ice Talons.*

CHAPTER TWENTY-FIVE

# The Lure of the Ember

In a glistening nest sparkling with frost and woven of ice shards, eight dark eggs shimmered.

"Beautiful, aren't they?" Nyra said with soft wonder. This particular fissure in the Ice Cliff Palace widened into a vast cave. Two dozen dragon owls from the Panqua Palace were sitting on more than a dozen similar nests. There were a few Pure Ones who had joined the broody forces. Everyone took turns nest-sitting. No one was excused, as Nyra had just explained to Tarn. It was now more important than ever, since four of the reinforcement broody owls had met an untimely death on their flight to the Ice Cliffs. But at least by that time all the eggs had been transported from the Gray Rocks. That they had not lost one egg during the skirmish with the kraals and gadfeathers was a miracle.

Occasionally now, one of the eggs would jiggle or rock back and forth just a bit.

"They'll get even darker," the Striga added. "By the time of the eclipse they will be completely black. The blackest black."

"How do you know?" Tarn asked.

"They always destroyed the eggs immediately after they were laid, but one was found once that had been secretly brooded, sequestered away, oh, a half century or more ago in the Dragon Court. It was, of course, immediately destroyed, but I caught a glimpse of it." A faraway look misted the Striga's pale yellow eyes. "I think that in some way I knew even then that it was my mission to see that such destruction might never happen again. And then when I actually had that first glimpse of the book in the library I felt disturbed, but I didn't know why. It was only when dear Nyra explained what she had seen in that book that it all came to me. Fit together so perfectly. And then she told me of her recovery in the Panqua Palace! Oh, and now we are so close. We are almost there! Four more nights of incubation and then a very short period after hatching, three nights at the most, and they shall be fit for battle."

"An honor, Striga," said one of the broodies. Then another added, "Until now our lives had no meaning."

"This is our destiny," another said as she moved back on the nest she had left temporarily so that Tarn could view the eggs.

"But what news do you bring me?" Nyra asked, turning to the Burrowing Owl. She had hardly given him a moment to speak since he had arrived and then she had launched into the broody schedule and how all must serve.

"Well, there is some good news," Tarn said carefully.

"And bad news as well?" Nyra's eyes narrowed.

"Not really bad news, Madame General. We may need to adjust our schedule."

"Now what do you mean by that?" Nyra asked.

"We have received word from several sources, including Kylor, the slipgizzle who defected from serving the Guardians, that the ember is now headed for the Beyond."

"The Beyond, not near the coast?" Striga said excitedly.

"They no longer seem headed toward the coast. It is as far from any water as one can imagine. You need not fear fighting any battles near salt water with the young hagsfiends," Tarn said, looking at the Striga. Relief seemed to sweep through the ice cave.

"That is good. The hatchling hagsfiends will mature quickly, but it's best to avoid salt water."

"And what is the business about a different schedule?" Nyra asked.

"Well, some say the ember will be there in a week."

"A week is fine. We'll be ready," Nyra replied.

"But others say that the ember is there now," Tarn replied.

"Now?" Nyra screeched, and she and the Striga both wilfed in alarm.

"Yes, but only temporarily. It will be taken to another secret location, most likely the Middle Kingdom."

"The Middle Kingdom?" the Striga exclaimed.

"You mean that we must act now?" Nyra said.

"Indeed, Madame General. I have already alerted our forces in the Kuneer to commence invasion maneuvers."

"But you had no authority to do that!" Nyra barked.

"But General, you were not there. We cannot afford to lose any time."

Nyra had swelled to twice her normal size.

"Tarn did the right thing!" the Striga hissed.

"Are you both turning on me?" Nyra raged.

"Calm yourself, Madame General." The Striga spoke urgently. Sometimes he wondered how this owl had become the leader she was. She acted purely on her impulses for power without ever reflecting on strategy. No wonder she had been defeated in every encounter with the Guardians, even those when she had enjoyed the advantage of superior forces. "This is no time to argue about silly protocols of command. If this war comes earlier, we must be prepared. If the ember is in the Beyond and if there is the threat of it being removed, we need to be able to act quickly."

"But what are we to do? These eggs are close but not close enough to hatching. We were counting on a hags force to help us seize the ember."

"They will hatch. Not as quickly as we might like, but when they do, they will come. This war is not going to be over in one night. But we must be ready with the forces that we can muster right now." The Striga said calmly.

He turned to the broodies. "Can you do double shifts? In other words, can we count on some of you to join us now in this fight? Elab, you are large, could you sit two ice nests at a time?"

"Oh, I think I could sit three if need be."

"Good. If we can cut our broody force in half that gives us eighteen more owls to fly with us in the Striga Force!" His pale eyes glittered brightly like translucent suns.

It galled Nyra no end — this "Striga Force" business. But she had decided not to argue with him over the name. They were only a part of the Pure Ones, and the Pure Ones were her army. Nyra might be impulsive, but she had learned how to pick her battles.

"Yes, yes, I see what you mean," Nyra said slowly. Her gizzard was twitching madly. The ember so near! And in a sense, so safe, for it was far from the water. The dragon owls need not fear the salt water, and when the hagsfiends finally hatched and were ready, they, too, would be safe. She imagined the horror in the Guardians' eyes when the sky above the volcanoes would suddenly darken as scores upon scores of hagsfiends flew over. "You're right. We must leave now, immediately. I shall send a message to Kuneer to begin advancing toward our mustering point, where I will meet them and resume my command of the Tytonic Union of Pure Ones." Nyra said these last five words in a measured voice and looked steadily at the Striga. *Now* that *is the name of an army,* she thought. "And from there to the Beyond, to the front."

"To the front," echoed the Striga.

## CHAPTER TWENTY-SIX

# A Slink Melf Swims On

They were heading to the Ice Palace, Namara in the lead. She had led two dozen wolves of her clan as far as possible over the land route from Broken Talon Point. At the edge of the Bitter Sea, she plunged in, striking out straight across it until she and her followers had climbed out on the other shore where the H'rathghar glacier commenced. One more water passage, across the Bay of Fangs, and they would have almost arrived at their destination: the Ice Talons, where she would home in on the target. She reflected now on all that had occurred since the polar bear Sveep had visited her. The news then had been alarming: Nyra, in collusion with this strange blue owl, the one called the Striga, of whom the wolves of the Beyond had only heard ominous rumors and who, for a brief time, had gained such power over Coryn. So it was with great relief when Coryn himself had sought her out a moon cycle after the visit from Sveep. By that time, she had already met with the other wolves of the Beyond to alert them that trouble might be brewing in the owl kingdom. The wolf clans all had a deep, abiding hatred of Nyra. Twice they had had confrontations with her. The first time was at the Sacred Ring, when Coryn had retrieved the ember and Nyra had made a desperate attempt to wrest it from him. But Namara (who was then known as Gyllbane) with the help of Hamish, had managed to prevent her succeeding. The second encounter was at the end of the Tunnel of Despair in the canyonlands at the Battle of the Book, the battle in which the she-wolf had lost her only son, Cody. The depth of Namara's loathing for this owl was unfathomable. Her only regret was that Nyra would not be in the Ice Palace with those heinous eggs so that she could personally put an end to her, too.

But she must rid herself of such distracting thoughts. Her mission was clear. The clan of the MacNamaras was to first destroy the eggs that would hatch the hagsfiends and then, if possible, to kill the Dragon Court owls who were brooding and guarding them. Coryn had selected them for this mission for three reasons: The first was their extraordinary sense of smell, which was vastly superior to that of owls. So although the intricate passages behind the walls of the ice cliffs that led deep into the Ice Palace were seemingly impenetrable,

Coryn realized that with their extraordinary olfactory sense, the wolves were the best suited to find the path to the eggs. He remembered reading in the legends of the stench of hagsfiends. Surely their eggs would bear traces of that malodorous scent, and surely Namara and her clan wolves could find them. The second reason Coryn had chosen the MacNamara clan was that they were the fiercest of all the clans. Many creatures who have endured cruelty become as abusive as their abusers — but not the wolves of Namara's clan. They were exceedingly tough but had a profound sense of justice and mercy. And the third reason to dispatch these wolves as a slink melf was their unparalleled tactical intuition. Before Coryn had come to this decision he reread the chapter in the legend *The Coming of Hoole* that described when Grank had taken the young king to the Beyond to learn from Fengo. Under Fengo he witnessed the genius of wolves on the hunt. Coryn, too, had been reflecting on this tactical brilliance for some time now. It was what led Coryn to seek Namara.

The wolves were in the water again after leaving the eastern shore of the H'rathghar glacier. Namara now turned into the straits of the Ice Talons. She was at the head of the byrrgis. It was a basic formation reconfigured for water passage. In this way they "broke track" in the water in much the same way they broke track when hunting in deep snow. At exactly the same moment, all the five wolves in this front rank detected the first tendril of the foul odor seeping from a fissure in the ice wall. Namara quickly did a wind check and calculated that this fissure must be catching a back draft from behind the cliff. This back draft would lead them to the schneddenfyrrs.

Almost undetectably, a series of signals passed among the wolves. They clambered out of the water and up the narrow ledges that rimmed the strait of the Ice Cliffs and began searching out possible entryways. Meticulous in their scent markings, each wolf left a coded trail for the next wolf of the clan to follow as they began splitting off toward different entrances into the ice cliffs.

Coryn had told Namara that this war — the War of the Ember — would be fought on many fronts. And that the first front and the most vital was here in the Ice Talons. He had told Namara and her clan of the legends, of how the wolves had defeated the hagsfiends in the Desert of Kuneer. Coryn's words stirred an ancient clan memory and a ferocious pride within them. It was said that wolves were very superstitious and often distrustful. Namara knew this was their reputation. Perhaps it was true. She would never argue that it wasn't, but now, as something deep within her stirred, she wondered if it was not so much superstition as this memory, this deep clan memory. She could almost feel that battle from one thousand years before in the desert. She narrowed her eyes and saw a thin stream of green light score the ice walls. "Cast your green! Cast your green!" It was an ancient voice from ancient times, the time of the legends.

There was a terrible shriek. Then an immense flapping sound. It was Blair. Her ear had been ripped from her head and was dangling over her eye. Her mouth gushed blood. The ice passage was turning red. Blue feathers spun through frigid air, and blades of moonlight slashed through the maelstrom of blood and feathers and the fetid muck of monstrous eggs. And so the first front in the War of the Ember opened.

CHAPTER TWENTY-SEVEN

# The Second Front

High over the Ice Talons two divisions of owls scraped across the nearly full-shine moon, heading in a southwesterly direction. Some were gaudily festooned in colorfully dyed feathers. They were the kraals. Although not the cleverest fighters, they were dangerous when unified by strong sympathies. The other division was composed of gadfeathers. They had set aside their usual beads and berries and now, like the kraals, carried short blades in their talons. After the atrocities of the massacre at the Gray Rocks these owls were eager to join the Guardian's forces and were proud to be led by Madame Plonk. The fame of the singer of the great tree was widespread in the Northern Kingdoms from which she had originally come. She was something of a folk hero. The kraals, always impressed with trappings of beauty, found her alluring, and the gadfeathers were in awe of her voice. That she held a charismatic charm for both groups rather astonished her.

* * *

A new wind was building. Rain and sleet slashed the darkness and, in the Beyond, thunderbolts stabbed the sky as flashes from the volcanoes ripped the night. But in the sheltered inlet, where the Sea of Vastness first broke on the rugged coast of the Beyond, a reunion was taking place.

Three Great Gray Owls perched on a rocky outcropping, speechless, their gizzards quivering. The two older owls were staring at the face of what was unmistakably the brother they had thought was lost forever. And Twilight blinked in amazement. "I thought I was an only owlet. I thought I was alone."

"And we thought you had died . . . with Mum."

"Me, die!" Twilight almost shouted. "But . . . but I honestly never thought, never dreamed I had a brother — two brothers! I . . . I . . ." he stuttered. "I'm not alone." He shook his head in wonder. Then he lofted himself wildly into the air. "I am not alone! I got me two bros!"

The world in that moment brimmed with the joy that flowed from the three owls. Once more the brothers recounted how they had met up with Soren and Wensel.

"You chased off Tarn, that bad-butt Burrowing Owl!" Twilight screeched gleefully.

"We know him and his ways. We've been out in the desert for years." Tavis turned to Digger. "No offense, but we can excavate as good as any Burrowing Owl."

"But they never got us," Cletus added. Soren, Gylfie, and Digger all blinked. Soren stepped forward.

"What do you mean they never got you?" Soren asked.

"The Pure Ones, and that blue owl. They've been recruiting troops out there for Glaux knows how long now."

"What?" Soren was stunned. "How? Nyra has nothing. What is she promising them?"

"A new kingdom," Tavis said matter-of-factly.

"What?" Gylfie flew right up to the two Great Grays. "A new kingdom? Where? How?"

"The one they call the Middle Kingdom. The one the blue owl comes from. He promises them a palace filled with jewels, servants, great splendors. And power."

"It's the same tactic that Theo used to get the hagsfiends out of the Hoolian world," Soren said.

"But why did we never hear of this until now? Why didn't our slipgizzle there say anything?"

"Oh, that Sooty Owl?" Cletus asked.

"Yes, Kylor. That's his name. Kylor."

"They bought him off," Tavis replied.

"How many of them are there?" Soren asked. The

two brothers looked at each other and blinked. And cocked their heads this way and that.

"Just a rough estimate," Digger said.

"Oh, nine hundred or so."

"What?" the owls gasped and instantly wilfed.

"Not more than a thousand."

"And we're supposed to find that comforting?" Gylfie gasped. "And what are we — all told — five hundred owls?"

"And now they are all probably heading toward the Beyond because of the ember!" Twilight exploded.

"Calm down! Calm down!" Soren said.

At that moment a messenger arrived. It was Clover. "Finding you was a pain in the gizzard!" The Barn Owl looked weary and the fringes of her primaries were storm-tattered. "I thought you'd be at the Wolf's Fang, but then I heard some wing beats in this direction."

"What's happening? You have an update?"

"Let me catch my breath." Within half a minute Clover had recovered her composure. Gylfie was thoughtfully preening the Barn Owl's fringes, which seemed to calm her. "All right. Enemy troops are heading toward the Beyond. They should be arriving in two nights. They are streaming out of Kuneer."

"Any sign of enemy movement in the Northern Kingdoms?"

"No, not yet. But our allied forces are definitely mustering," Clover replied.

Digger took a step forward. "Why no sign of the enemy if they are, as we believe, in the Ice Cliff Palace? If they'd seen our allied forces in the Northern Kingdoms, wouldn't they come?"

"Not if they are busy brooding a haggish force of their own," Gylfie said.

"Yes, of course," Digger replied.

"There have been rumors of Nyra flying out of the Northern Kingdoms, flying south to a mustering point to lead her troops into the Beyond. We suspect the Striga will follow with dragon owls and . . ." Clover hesitated. She could hardly bring herself to say the word. "And hagsfiends within hours of their hatching."

Just minutes before this report from Clover, Soren had counseled them all to calm down but now his own gizzard was in a complete tumult, grinding and lurching as if there was a storm raging in there. He swallowed hard on a rising pellet. He pressed his beak shut and squinted. *Concentrate! Concentrate!* There was a flickering in his brain. Every Band member fell silent and stared at Soren. They knew this posture. Beak clamped, eyes slitted, he was turning his head in small circles as he did when scooping up sound. Except it was not sound he sought but ideas, memories. "Gareth's Keep." Soren said the two words distinctly.

"Gareth's Keep," Gylfie repeated. "The fortress in the Battle of Little Hoole where Strix Struma . . . That was years ago."

"Exactly!" Soren's eyes now blazed. "The Keep was almost impenetrable. Before the Battle of Little Hoole, word came of an invasion by the enemy, the Ice Talons League. Although vastly outnumbered, the troops of the Northern Kingdoms defeated the invaders by luring them into the narrow pass of Gareth's Keep. It is one of the most famous battles in Hoolian history.

"We can do what Strix Struma did thirty years ago: use the natural terrain."

"What terrain are you talking about?" Ruby asked.

"The yondos!" Soren and Gylfie both said at once.

The yondos were the strange rock formations that rose, writhing and twisting, from the volcanic landscape of the Beyond. The two largest yondos were called the Hot Gates of the Beyond because they were massive and flanked the entrance to the Sacred Ring of Volcanoes. A mountain ridge backed them up.

The words tumbled out of Gylfie's beak in a rush.

"We can do what they did at Little Hoole — block their passage to the Sacred Ring. Trap them in between the two yondos in the narrowest air corridors and attack in waves just as they get into the passage. There will be no room for them to maneuver."

"Ruby!" Soren turned to the Short-eared Owl.

"Yes, sir!" Soren blinked. He still couldn't get used to this normally ruddy owl with her new blondish-hued feathers. "Take this message to Coryn — by now he should be at the Sacred Ring of Volcanoes."

"What's the message?"

"'Gareth's Keep.'" No need for code. He'll know what I mean. Coryn is a student of history and he's read every word written on the Battle of Little Hoole."

Ruby took off, a blur darting through the night. It was probably the fastest flight any owl had ever made in such miserable weather. At this time of the year the Hoolestar rose in the northeast and began its westerly passage. It had hardly flickered over the horizon when Ruby arrived at the Sacred Ring. She was exhausted and gasped not two words but six: "Gareth's Keep. Enemy force one thousand."

Coryn instantly knew the meaning of her words.

And thus a second front opened in the War of the Ember.

CHAPTER TWENTY-EIGHT

# The Hot Gates of the Beyond

Wolf scouts from the Beyond and owl scouts from various stations were dispatched immediately to report on the progress of the enemy troops that had been surging out of Kuneer. In relays they reported back to Coryn, who was already established in the Beyond. Nyra was reported to have arrived with an advance unit of Pure Ones at the northern border of Ambala, where they had encountered and skirmished with units of Ambalan owls. The casualties were low. And the Pure Ones were now slicing across the northern corner of the canyonlands, choosing a longer route rather than fighting a headwind that would exhaust them.

In the meantime, Coryn looked out upon his own troops from his perch on top of the westernmost yondo, his back to the direction from which the enemy owls would approach. The Band perched on either side of him. He looked out at the harsh land between where he perched and the Sacred Ring. The Guardians numbered five hundred owls all told. That number, however, did not account for the other animal species from the Northern Kingdoms, which had been streaming in at a steady rate.

The Strix Struma Strikers needed no introduction to the strategy of Gareth's Keep. The late founder of their unit, Strix Struma herself, had devised it. Behind them was the flame squadron, then the fighting companies from the Northern Kingdoms: the Frost Beaks, the Glauxspeed unit, and an entire division of Kielian snakes who would fight aboard their broad backs. Behind the Glauxspeed were the gadfeathers and the kraals jointly commanded by Madame Plonk. Beyond them, rippling in the dark night like a broad white river, were the polar bears. Finally, lurking around the edges of this mass of creatures, were the wolves of the Beyond in stealth units, or phyrngs, of less than a dozen wolves each, known for the speed and surprise of their attacks.

All in all, it was an incredible assortment of creatures. Never before had such disparate species been brought together to fight as one army. But could these animals so bound to earth vanquish an enemy that soared in the sky? Company by company, the landscape beneath the volcanoes became a solid mass of animals from all parts of the Hoolian world.

Coryn glanced at the unit that Doc Finebeak had just led to the slopes. The crows! He blinked, for among them he saw the white feathers of seagulls. Leaning toward Soren, he whispered, "Are those what I think they are, in among the crows?"

"I believe so. Rumor has it that Doc Finebeak had recruited seagulls as well. Together, it is known as the Black and White Brigade. But among the seagulls, their unit is called 'The Splat.' They specialize in splat attacks." Soren paused. "And that means what you think it means!"

"Great Glaux!" Coryn murmured, then began his address to the troops. "Owls, wolves, bears, crows, seagulls. Colliers, Rogue smiths, gadfeathers, kraals — This is a historic moment in the history of our Hoolian world. We have forgotten those things that separate us into species and have come to fight as one. Creatures of honor, creatures of dignity, who value freedom. It makes no difference if we are of fur or feather, earth or sky. You are here because you want to defend your dens, your nests, your ice caves, and because you would not want to be any other place." He paused and looked out into the sky. The storm had abated, the sky had cleared, and an amazing sight was melting out of the night. Crisp white marks, rather like punctuation points in the night, marked with bright slashes of orange. "Great Glaux!" Coryn said, astounded. Fifty or more puffins were landing in a tightly packed formation. They made their way to the front ranks just below where Coryn perched.

"Reporting for duty, sir!" Dumpy the Fifteenth said. A frozen fish dropped from his mouth as he spoke.

Coryn continued speaking. "You are here," he said, looking now directly at Dumpy. "Because you are smart, brave, tough creatures, loyal creatures, good creatures in a world that is threatened by violence. Yes, it is true. Some of us will die. But death must not be feared. Death in time comes to all creatures. Yes, every animal is frightened in its first battle. If that animal claims not to be frightened, then that animal is a liar. The real hero is the animal who fights even though scared. That is courage. There can be no courage without fear. We are all Rogue smiths of courage. We extract the metal of courage from the ore of raw fear. You will transform your fear, and thus yourself. And finally, you will save a kingdom.

"We are going to pin this enemy between these two yondos, these two Hot Gates. And then we are going to come at those Pure Ones in waves and never let up. War is bloody. You are going to have to spill their blood or they will spill yours. We are few, they are many, but in this land of the Beyond we shall set a standard of valor unmatched in the long history of the Hoolian world. And when you are old and gray, when you are grandmothers and grandfathers and your pups or chicks or cubs ask what you did, you can say, 'Child, I flew, I ran, I galloped, I fought in the Great Hoolian Army led by the Guardians of Ga'Hoole!'"

And then it was not but an hour later that the sky began to shake, not with thunder but the sound of a thousand wings beating the air. An enemy army of owls so vast, so massive that it was nearly unimaginable.

Coryn flew to the high tip of the yondo, and Soren to another, both brandishing ice scimitars. A signal was given and the dire wolves rushed out in classic double byrrgis formation. Though they stood only half as tall as the polar bears, they began leaping straight up to a distance that was twice the bears' height as they herded the first ranks of the approaching enemy owls and funneled them through the two gates to trap them. Colliers of the Sacred Ring swooped down, launching thousands upon thousands of burning embers. The sky sizzled with the red-hot trajectories inscribed against the black night. Behind them, like a massive solid wall, a phalanx of polar bears reared up. The attacking owls that slipped through the ember grid were batted out of the sky by the bears with their massive paws.

"We are holding them off!" Twilight cried. He and his two brothers together formed a flying wedge that blasted through the capricious winds, heading off any owls who broke through these first barriers of the ember grid and the polar bear phalanx. Some of the enemy did breach these barriers. But the three brothers chased them relentlessly. "Tarn, you fool," cried Tavis, for Tarn the Burrowing Owl, with a squad of a dozen owls, was advancing on Coryn. The three brothers flew and fought together as if they had been doing it all their lives.

*Chase that tail! Let him wail.*
*Slug him, bug him,*
*That pile of splat.*
*Mow him down, the dirty rat.*

The three chased Tarn and his small contingent. Meanwhile, Soren and Ruby and other members of the flame squadron pressed, with burning branches, a larger contingent of Pure Ones that was trying to breach the eastern flank. They were not having much success.

Half of those enemy troops had managed to slip by them, but suddenly, as the dawn was approaching, tinting the horizon a cool pink against the hot red of battle, a loud roar went up. It was the Strix Struma Strikers under the command of Otulissa, flying in her late mentor's position on the windward flank. They had just routed a sub squad that had broken into the armory. Quentin, the quartermaster in charge, an elderly Barred Owl, had tried to hold them off but he was injured. Soren caught all this as Otulissa screamed by him shouting commands: "Vacuum transport needed at armory!" A half dozen sky medics led by Cleve flew by seconds later.

Coryn raced to the armory. "Hold on, old fellow! Hold on!" He crouched over Quentin, who had collapsed in the cave. A wolf was helping by cleaning up the wound to his port wing.

"Coryn," gasped the old Barred Owl.

"Don't try to talk now, Q. You have to save your strength."

"No, Coryn. Listen to me. Dawn is coming. I have an idea. These ice shields. They're cloud ice, you know." Cloud ice was ice that was opaque because of trapped air bubbles.

"Q, you shouldn't be talking."

"I'm not hurt badly. Not as bad as it looks. You've got to listen to me!" There was a fierceness in his amber eyes. "That cloud ice. I've been experimenting with it. I got an idea when this wolf was licking up my blood. . . . what's his name?"

"What's your name?" Coryn asked, swiveling his head toward a gray-and-black wolf.

"Patches, sir." His left forepaw was deformed. Obviously, a gnaw wolf who would have been destined for the Sacred Watch if the ember had been buried in the volcano. Coryn felt a stirring in his gizzard. The ember itself was tucked away right now in the armory cave, one bucket amid many toward the back. These buckets were only to be broken out if they were low on coals at the ignition stations and only with Coryn's explicit permission. It would have been easy perhaps to return the ember in the thick of battle, but before he did it he had plans for it. To himself, Coryn called those plans Operation Death Lure. He would lure Nyra and the Striga into an absolutely indefensible position. There would be no escape. If the ember could be the instrument through which these two owls met their deaths, then it was worth all the grief it had caused.

Coryn turned his attention back to Quentin. "His name is Patches. Now, what do you want to tell him?"

"Patches, young'un," Quentin said softly. "You got brothers? Sisters?"

"Yes, sir. But you know, they don't pay me much heed, sir."

"Now why'd that be?" Quentin asked. Coryn was ready to explode. He did not feel Quentin should be wasting his energy. He could see that the old Barred Owl was growing weaker.

"Because I am lame."

"Well, I'm not shunning you. You're important. You cleaned up my blood with that tongue of yours. It's a rough tongue. Good for polishing. You go get your brothers and your sisters. And you tell them that the quartermaster, that's me, Quentin, Barred Owl. *Strix varia* . . ."

"For Glaux's sake, you don't have to give your species, Q. Save your breath."

But Q paid him no attention. His amber eyes were set on Patches' green eyes. "Get those wolves now. In the back of the cave are four dozen ice shields. Start licking them. Lick them until they glow, until they are burnished, then set them out." Painfully, he turned his head now toward Coryn. He closed his eyes and spoke. "I want those shields to flash, flash brilliantly, blindingly . . . do . . . you . . . understand? Dawn's about to break. The armory faces east — the rising sun. Do . . . you . . . understand?"

Coryn did! And it was just then he noticed the trickle of blood coming from behind Q's head. He heard Patches gasp, for the wolf saw it at the same time. "Don't lick it." Q said in a low, rough whisper. "Save your spit, lad." There was a rough billowy hiccup sound, then quiet. A slight breeze seemed to pass through the cave. *Gone, he's gone!* Coryn thought. *The old quartermaster is . . .* But before he could complete the thought, Patches was racing from the cave.

## CHAPTER TWENTY-NINE

# The Last Glow

From her command position outside the yondos, Nyra squinted into the rising sun. The glare was ferocious. Not only did the sun burn, but two east-facing volcanoes, Dunmore and Morgan, had begun to erupt sporadically. The glare of the flames intensified. The battleground became quiet for the moment. "We shall hold off for now. We need to regain our strength and wait for reinforcements," Nyra shouted to her troops.

Next to her the Striga perched. He leaned over and whispered to her, "Just eighteen more hours, and then, my dear . . ."

Nyra once again silently railed at the intimacy of the Striga's tone. It had no place on a battlefield. "Yes, eighteen more hours until the great hatching. And you feel the first flight could come almost immediately?"

"Yes, I am certain."

The hours of the day crept by slowly. In each camp the leaders, though exhausted, could not rest. Coryn was in deep discussion with his uncle and the rest of the Band.

"So," Soren said, turning to Hamish. "As far as we know there's been no news from the slink melf as to whether they arrived at the Ice Talons."

"I doubt they would send any word back. The only way we would know is if someone spotted Namara and her clan of wolves swimming across the Everwinter Sea and up the straits."

"So we must simply wait," Digger said ominously.

A young lieutenant from the Frost Beaks appeared. It was a Scops Owl, tiny, with delicate talons. "A message from the enemy: They want to parley."

"It could be a trick," Otulissa said immediately.

"Could be, yes," Coryn said. But he was anxious to hear what they had to say. Was it time for Operation Death Lure? He swiveled his head toward Hamish, who since the war had begun, had become an indispensable advisor because of his knowledge of the territory.

"We can send a wolf guard with you. I would advise meeting them on the high ridgeline just outside the Hot Gates," Hamish said.

"No," Coryn said. "I will take only my uncle, Soren."

* * *

Coryn and Soren flew to the ridge. Nyra and the Striga faced them on another ridge.

"Listen to me," Nyra shouted out. "Do not think that because we are outside the Hot Gates of the Sacred Ring we have retreated. Clever of you to polish those ice shields. But the dawn dies as the sun rises. And reinforcements come. By noon tomorrow your flame squadron, your Strix Struma Strikers, your Frost Beaks will be finished because our hagsfiends will blot out the sun and you will die."

"Then we shall fight you in the shade!" Coryn replied.

"Be sensible. Lay down your weapons." The Striga stepped forward on the perch.

"Come and get them," Coryn said in a deadly voice that rang out. A wild cheer went up from the colliers of the Sacred Ring. "Our parley is over!"

As they flew back, Soren glanced at the shields. Nyra was right. This trick would only work at dawn, but he thought, *Supposing we could form a phalanx of ice shields, overlapping ice shields that could be strategically moved? A mobile unit?* The hagsfiends' most powerful weapon was their fyngrot, the deadly yellow glare that streamed from their eyes, which induced an instant paralysis and caused its victims to go yeep. But what if the poisonous yellow glare could be turned back on the attackers?

"We need Otulissa!" Soren said. "I have an idea."

The fighting resumed shortly after the parley, but there was enough time to arrange flying phalanx. It was composed of the largest owls and captained by the eagles Zan and Streak, who had accompanied the Ambalan owls to the front. The eagles were large enough to manipulate two shields each in their talons and another in their beaks. They would make up the center span of the phalanx. Gylfie flew as the coxswain, or steer bird. Her task was to call out the shifting positions in accordance with the hagsfiends' movements and the wind. The flying ice shield would have to be navigated through the sky, and the tiny Elf Owl's navigation skills were unequaled. She was precisely the owl for this job.

As the day dwindled into night, a short cease-fire was called and the moon rose, full shine in its cycle. This night would bring the eclipse. The tension among the animals increased. An unnerving silence settled on the battlefield, a sense of unreality as all waited for that moment when the earth's shadow would creep across that of the moon, first just nibbling away at its luminous roundness, then gnawing great chunks from it, and finally swallowing it. Would those dark eggs in the ice nests begin to hatch? After a thousand years, would the hagsfiends slip back once more into the world of owls?

The quiet thickened. "They will hatch. They will come!" a voice screeched. It was the Striga who spoke. The night grew blacker and blacker as the earth's shadow slid on its inexorable path across the moon, and into the darkness he whispered, "And when the moon shines again, there will be a new order and I shall rule with my queen, Nyra, the supreme, all-powerful Empress of the Tytonic Union of Pure Ones."

There was an enormous shree. Coryn recognized it as the voice of his mother, Nyra. She and the Striga were both drunk on the vision of their own impending omnipotence. Coryn thought, *They are defying Glaux. They believe they are Glaux, and that is their fatal flaw!*

While every creature on the field of battle tipped its head to watch the moon, Coryn slipped back to the armory. There were still stains of Quentin's blood on the cave's floor, though his body had been removed. Coryn dipped his beak into one of the countless buckets, extracted the Ember of Hoole, and, under the cover of the complete blackness of the eclipse, flew toward Hrath'ghar, the very same volcano from which he had taken the ember many moon cycles before. This, Coryn knew, was the most important mission of his life. Many thoughts streamed through his mind. His gizzard quivered with a storm of sensations. It seemed not that long ago that he had retrieved the ember. *Now,* Coryn thought, *I am returning it.* His greatness had begun with the ember. *But what I do now is greater. This I know.* And Coryn's gizzard tingled with a joy that he had never before known. He remembered vividly that day when he had retrieved the ember. He had whistled out of Hrath'ghar's crater with a blazing rainbow of sparks streaming from the ember. The cheers, the wild joy that swept through the air! Within a space of seconds, he had gone from outcast to hero, from the son of tyrants to king of the most noble owls on earth. But now Coryn knew that it was better to release than to retrieve, to yield rather than capture. He neared the rim of Hrath'ghar, then he was in the deep cauldron of its crater. He swooped and flew close to the leaping flames within the crater, which suddenly died down as if to welcome him. Bubbles of lava boiling to the surface popped open like dark mouths awaiting the gift they were about to receive. Coryn dropped the ember quietly, closed his eyes, and felt, despite the fierce heat of the volcano, a cool breeze. A profound relief swept through his gizzard. "At last," he murmured. *At last!* But he did not linger. The fighting would resume as soon as the moon's light returned. He would be ready.

At the same moment Coryn dropped the ember into the crater, the first contingent of the blue owls of the Danyar Division arrived. The horizon was touched with a strange blue tinge. So startling was the spectacle of the legions of iridescent owls that there was a lull in the fighting. All eyes were trained on the horizon to the far west. No one noticed Coryn flying over the volcano save one: Hamish, who scampered from a wolf hole dug near the front lines and walked almost casually in the direction Coryn was flying. He did not want to attract attention. But almost as soon as Coryn had taken the ember, Hamish had sensed it, for he had been a member of the Watch. It was like a distant call, a summoning. He felt his leg begin to grow crooked again and the limp return. But he felt his body grow stronger, as was the way with gnaw wolves of the Sacred Watch. His muscles and sinews swelled. Despite his limp, a litheness suffused his body. He was the new Fengo of the Sacred Watch. The keenest, most alert, most powerful wolf became the Fengo. He raised his snout. The she-winds, those winds unique to the Sacred Ring, had begun to blow. He climbed to the top of one of the towering mounds of gnaw bones. These mounds, or cairns, encircled the volcanoes of the Sacred Ring. When the ember lay buried in a volcano, atop each cairn a gnaw wolf sat its watch.

Hamish looked. He saw his old teacher, Banquo, returning to the mound next to his, and then came Fleance, and Donalbain. *They know!* thought Hamish. Banquo gave him a slight nod as if to say, "'Tis back." His tilted green eyes sparkled as the moon emerged from earth's shade. One minute passed, then another, then an hour, and yet there was nary a sign of a hagsfiend. But then in the glare of the full-shine moon, an alarm went out. Wolves, but not those of the Sacred Watch, began to howl.

Hamish was suddenly alert. His ears pricked forward. He tipped his head toward the sky, which was streaked with moonlight. But still no hagsfiends.

"Who is the traitor?" someone roared. Then the MacNamara clan stormed in. Namara had Cato MacHeath by the throat. She threw his body down. "They are coming. The Pure Ones. Hecate showed them the old caribou pass, round back of the yondos. They come now. See them."

"But no hagsfiends?" Coryn had landed beside the wolf.

"No." Namara immediately prostrated herself before her commander, in the position of submission. "There are no hagsfiends. Nor will there be. Eggs destroyed. Mission accomplished, Your Majesty." Alighting next to her were two owls, Braithe, a Whiskered Screech from Ambala, and his mate, Fiona. Braithe now stepped forward. "The wolves of Namara fought splendidly, sir."

The world resolved itself into a velvety darkness. The she-winds died to a whisper and all that could be heard was the crackling of lava bubbles in the volcanoes' craters. There was a sudden beating of wings. And a shrill cry from Nyra, "Two thousand strong we are now. Surrender the ember and we shall go in peace."

"Never!" Coryn shouted back.

*Why doesn't he say that the ember is gone? That it is deep in the crater?* Hamish wondered. *What is he trying to do?* And then it struck Hamish. Coryn wanted to use it as the lure. The ember might be buried, but Coryn had unfinished business. And this was, in a sense, the ember's last glow. *And,* Hamish thought as the reality dawned on him, *Coryn will never rest until he knows Nyra is dead.*

"Lay down the ember!" Nyra cried out.

And this time he replied, "Come and get it."

Coryn quickly seized a bonk coal. Where it came from, Hamish was not sure. Perhaps he had been carrying it all along. Hamish slid his green eyes toward the other gnaw wolves of the watch. *They know,* he thought. *They know.* Coryn might be able to fool Nyra, fool all the animals who had gathered, but not the wolves of the Watch. They knew that this ember that Coryn now held in his talon was not the Ember of Hoole.

"The moon shines bright! There are no hagsfiends. Dispatch the ice phalanx." Coryn whispered the command. In the meantime, there were the gusty sounds of the lethal Breaths of Qui as the first Danyar legions began their rout of entire squads of Pure Ones.

There was a small blur as Gylfie whizzed through the air and took up her position. "We shall capture the moon!" she cried out. There was a roar of approval as the flying phalanx took wing and suddenly the night was bright as the overlapping ice shields caught the light from the moon and flung it back into the eyes of the assaulting troops.

Ice missiles sliced the dark while the seagulls led by Doc Finebeak strafed the air just above the Pure Ones with round after round of splat. The enemy was confused and blinded by glaring light and seagull poop. It took three Pure Ones to give chase to one Hoolian owl. Bubo had taken over the position of the fallen quartermaster and was quickly issuing black ice goggles to protect the eyes of Hoolian owls from the glare. Fritha was overseeing ignition stations for the owls that fought with fire. Trees of lightning spread their crackling limbs in the dark sky as an electrical storm shattered the night and thunderbolts stabbed the darkness.

Coryn, meanwhile, was luring Nyra closer and closer with the ember. Twilight and Soren were trying to protect him, serving as a flanking guard, but Coryn was so quick it was hard to keep up with him or anticipate where he might dart next. With the ember in his beak, a burning branch in his port talon, and an ice scimitar in his starboard one, he was a fearsome sight. But no more fearsome than Nyra.

Twilight's gizzard seized as he saw a yellow light begin to seep from her eyes. "Great Glaux," he whispered. "Is she . . . ?" He dared not complete the thought.

Yes. She was becoming a hagsfiend before their very eyes. The yellow glare grew stronger. Soren saw that Coryn had begun to fly unevenly. "It's the fyngrot!" Did he shout that or did someone else?

Coryn realized what was happening. He was more frightened than he had ever been before. He could taste the bile of his fear. He could feel his muscles locking. He began to stagger in flight. But when he was the most frightened, he stilled his thoughts, reached deep inside himself to the bottom of his gizzard, and from it he extracted the "ore" of his raw fear. *I shall smelt this into courage. I will fight on with my eyes closed if I have to.*

At the same time, Coryn had another realization: that although the ember was hidden away and the world was safer, he still had not accomplished all he had set out to do. And if he did not live to be part of that new safer world . . . well, was not his life a small price to pay for this peace? He knew that he was staring death in the face. And that face was the face of his mother. She had reverted to her true nature. And although his mother's blood might run through his veins, her nature was not his. He had found his true self in this War of the Ember.

All of his fears dissolved. He was prepared to fly into the wings of death. He had no links to life, no mate, no offspring. But he still had life itself and that he would give gladly, to ensure that Nyra never again tyrannized the world of owls. There would be no peace until she was destroyed. She would never give up. She would always be a threat. This must be the last fight. *It must end here,* he thought. He felt his gizzard throbbing now, not with pain or anxiety but excitement. He was over the crater of Hrath'ghar from where he had first retrieved the ember.

Soren watched as Coryn, who a minute before had been at his side, suddenly veered off. *What is he doing?* Soren wondered in alarm as he saw Coryn make a wild dash to the crater's edge. He was waving the ember, beckoning to Nyra. The rims of craters were notoriously dangerous. She-winds could erupt violently around them as cool air collided with the volcano's heat to create lethal shears and downdrafts. Was Coryn going to fight his mother at the crater's edge in the maelstrom of a she-wind? Soren saw Nyra fly directly toward Coryn. The young king was alone now. Twilight had flown off to another skirmish, where his two brothers were outnumbered. Coryn had no one to fight alongside him. Soren had no choice. He hurled himself toward Coryn in the wake of Nyra. If he could only catch up with the vile owl and finish her off! But she'd already reached the rim. He saw Coryn parry and then dive into a gap in the flames of the volcano. Soren blinked. It was an insanely perilous maneuver that Coryn had just executed. But it allowed Soren to slide into a flanking position close to his nephew's starboard wing.

"You shouldn't be here, Uncle."

"I can think of no better place than at your side." Before they knew it, Nyra had flown into the same space. They began circling one another. It was two against one. Still, it was difficult. The winds were strong, tumultuous. Blessedly, the she-winds had not started to blow. The volcano itself, however, was in a phase of active eruption. Sheets of flames rose like dancing curtains, a labyrinth of fire. And Coryn was leading Nyra deeper and deeper into the maze. Soren was gripped with a fear he had never known, even as a collier diving into forest fires. These flames were different. But he thought, *We are colliers, Coryn and I. Nyra is not! We can do this!* Deeper and deeper they flew into the very heart of the eruption, skimming the boiling red-black sea of the crater. Not only did they have to dodge flames but crashing waves of molten lava. *Why in the name of Glaux has Coryn lured Nyra to this location?* Then it suddenly dawned on Soren. *He thinks no enemy troops will follow.*

They arrived at a clear space where the tunnels of flames opened. And just at that same moment, there was a smear of blue. The Striga! The blue owl appeared suddenly through a gap in the wall of flames. He flew to Nyra's side. Nyra swelled in his presence. Soren saw her eyes brighten. *Great Glaux!* Yellow poured from her eyes for a second time during this long battle. Could she control it or did it happen without her willing it?

At that moment, Coryn flew toward both the owls, then went into a hover a short distance from his mortal enemies, his mother and the Striga. Soren felt his gizzard lock. Was he snagged in the fyngrot? He saw his nephew slowly extend his talon with the ember almost like an offering as he dipped down in obeisance. The she-winds started to blow and, like maverick tendrils shorn from the main body of the wind, gusts began to seep through the fissures between the flames, disturbing the already confusing air currents. In another two seconds, it would be nearly impossible to fly. Coryn knew he had to act now. He moved in on the two owls.

Tucked under his port wing, Soren carried an ice splinter. He watched carefully, hoping that Coryn could maneuver the owls so he could get a clear shot at either Nyra or the Striga. Suddenly, Soren realized that the ember Coryn held out was a counterfeit, and that the Striga and Nyra did not know this. They were transfixed by the ember. Nyra came closer and closer. *If she will only turn just a bit,* Soren thought, *I will have a clear shot at her.*

"At last, an obedient son," Nyra hissed as she flew closer, extending her own fire-clawed talon. And just as she took the ember, to draw her attention Soren shouted, "It's fake!" Her eyes opened in horror as she turned toward him, her chest exposed. *Now or never!* Soren launched the ice splinter directly at her chest. There was a small spurt of blood, then a gush. The splinter had buried itself deep in her heart. She looked again in horror, first at Soren and then Coryn. For a moment she seemed suspended between two columns of flames, and then she said, "You cheated me, your own mother."

"You dare call yourself my mother?" Coryn said evenly.

Nyra lurched forward. Soren thought he saw Coryn flinch.

The Striga rushed in and swept under Nyra. He was trying to support her from below. But suddenly, the she-winds were raking through the flames and the scalding waves from the lava sea were rising higher. In the next moment a crest of the lava sea broke and took her with it. The Striga had slid away in the nick of time. "Out of here! Coryn!" Soren cried. "We have to get out. The she-winds are building!"

"Follow him!" Coryn cried out. "Follow the Striga!"

"Let him go, Coryn! Let him go!"

"Never!" Coryn shouted. He was flying like an owl possessed. Soren would not let him give chase alone. But suddenly the air was clear. They were out from the hot fiery breath of the volcano and the tumult of the she-winds and yet . . . *My Glaux, I am flying through blood!* Soren thought. *Blood! How can this be?*

And then he saw it! The blood was streaming from Coryn's port wing. The wing hung at an odd angle. His flight was unbalanced. The Striga wheeled about and was advancing on Coryn.

"No!" screeched Soren. He roared in and, with the ancient battle claws of Ezylryb extended, raked off the head of the Striga. The blue head spun off in one direction, the body in another. But there was something else. The tawny bloodstained wing of a Barn Owl swirled almost lazily to the ground. "Coryn! Coryn!" Soren watched, his gizzard quaking as Coryn plummeted. Soren flew to him and, with his battle claws still extended, caught his nephew and cradled him in those claws as if he were a chick just out of the shell.

A strange stillness settled upon the battlefield. Had the fighting stopped? Soren did not know, did not care. He landed at the base of the volcano and laid Coryn gently among the embers. Suddenly, the Band was by his side. "He's hurt! Badly hurt!" Soren cried out.

"Uncle, I am dying."

"No!" Soren whispered.

Otulissa appeared with the torn-off wing. "No, Coryn! No!" She could not believe this was happening. Above the place where Coryn now lay, Otulissa had years before perched on an outcropping and watched in astonishment as young Coryn had retrieved the ember.

"Coryn," Otulissa said softly, "Cleve will come. He will mend you. Sew your wing back on."

"I am fine. I don't need wings where I am going."

He was so tired. Coryn looked up at the good noble owls gathered around him. The band, the Chaw of Chaws. They were all weeping, begging him to live. But he knew he was leaving them. *They will have years and years, but my time is here.* He was ready. The last thing he heard before losing consciousness was not the voices of the Band but the howling of the wolves. And yet they seemed not near but in some distant country.

*Don't worry,* he wanted to say. *Don't worry, Uncle.* But he felt as if he was already far away.

A messenger arrived. "The enemy has been routed, sir." Then he looked down and gasped. "The king?"

"The king is dead!" said Soren quietly.

Soren flew over and perched on the top of one of the great gates of the Beyond. He swiveled his head and surveyed the battlefield. *It's a miracle,* he thought softly. *We were but five hundred Guardians and yet creatures from all over joined us. Creatures who had never before fought together found a way.* He saw Doc Finebeak in the distance. He was tending to the birds in his Black and White Brigade. *Crows! Who would have ever thought we would have crows as allies? And seagulls?* His eyes scanned the splatterings of white gull poop that seemed everywhere. But how effective that flying splat had been in the final rout. *Perhaps they have less than noble digestive tracts but their gizzards proved true,* Soren thought.

Suddenly, there was a huge roar and the ground shook beneath them. The five volcanoes of the Sacred Ring began to erupt all at once. The wolves howled a warning for, although such occasions were rare, fire could sweep across the land and the sky would then become a sea of flames. Owls began to fly through the Hot Gates but Soren stayed perched. He knew in his gizzard that he must remain. And so apparently did the rest of the Band and Otulissa. When he looked about, the entire Chaw of Chaws was perched on the pinnacles of the Hot Gates. And as they watched, they saw a misty configuration that seemed improbable in the hot dry air begin to rise over the crater of Hrath'ghar.

"Look, it's growing brighter!" Otulissa said.

"Like stars almost," Gylfie whispered.

"Not *like* stars, they *are* stars!" Twilight said.

Soren could scarcely breath. "It's a new constellation, I think."

"It's a face — a Barn Owl's face. I swear it's Coryn's, but there is no scar," Digger said.

"No, of course not," Soren said. "He has been restored, just as the wolves of the Watch are mended when the ember is retrieved. So Coryn is mended in glaumora."

The din of the erupting volcanoes now quieted. The flames that had scratched the sky retreated. The she-winds stilled and the only sound to be heard now was the bubbling, crackling noises of the boiling lava in the five craters and the rising cries of the wolves.

"Soren," Gylfie said. "Soren, look around." She nodded her head toward the ring of volcanoes. Upon each cairn a wolf stood and stretched its long neck toward the sky and began to howl.

"The ember is back," he replied. "They mourn for their lost king and their lost lives."

"No, Soren. They are not so selfish as to mourn for themselves. They could have left the Watch during Coryn's reign. But listen to their song. It's not sad." The voices of the wolves grew louder. The wild, untamed song curled into the night. Namara trotted up to Soren. "It is the Song of the Monarch."

"Monarch? But the king is dead."

"There will be a new king, unembered but Glaux blessed."

"No!" Soren gasped.

"Yes," three voices said. He turned and looked at Gylfie, Twilight, and Digger perched before him.

"Now it is your time," Digger said. Twilight and Gylfie nodded. Another voice spoke. "Your time, Soren." It was Otulissa. Namara had fallen to her knees, her belly scraping the ground. A mighty roar rang out through the Sacred Ring. The polar bears leaped into the night. And the gadfeathers began to sing their song blending with that of the wolves.

"My king," a sweet familiar voice said. It was Pelli.

"Just your mate, my dear. That is all I need be in your eyes." Soren saw his own reflection in the dark mirrors of Pelli's eyes. His white face soot-streaked. A nick out of his tarnished beak. "A grimy old mate at that," he added.

"Oh, no, as fresh and gleaming as a long night in the time of the White Rain, Soren."

# Epilogue

In a hollow high up on the northwest side of the great tree, formerly the hollow of its most distinguished ryb, Ezylryb, Otulissa perched over the writing table while Cleve poked at the fire in the grate. She picked up a feather freshly plucked from her port wing. The port ones seemed to grow the best quills for writing. It was up to her now. She had been appointed the official historian of the tree. Dipping the point into the ink, she began to write.

AN EYEWITNESS ACCOUNT
THE WAR OF THE EMBER

*Before I begin a detailed narrative of the causes leading up to this war, with its strategies and tactics, permit me, dear reader, a few more personal comments on war itself. Many think of war as an exercise in tactical deployment, weapons, and training. War as work, in the grittiest and most mundane sense. Others think it a blood-drenched glamorous drama. But I would like to suggest that war is something else. It is perhaps essentially mysterious, for it requires courage in ways that are not only extraordinary but ultimately inspiring. An ordinary owl is suddenly called upon to do extraordinary things, and this the owl does! How is that explained? Perhaps in years to come, owls and other creatures might visit that battleground in Beyond the Beyond where this War of the Ember was fought and our good King Coryn perished along with many other animals — ordinary animals who died courageously, as well. So I ask you, who are strangers to me, to pass on this truth: Tell all that pause at that hallowed ground, that here lie Guardians. For Guardians they all were, be they owls, wolves, seagulls, puffins, bears, snakes, or crows. They came together in the dark and fearsome glare of three cursed nights to fight and to die obedient to the oaths of the Great Ga'Hoole Tree. Have them know that this tree is no myth, though a mystery it may be, for the courage it has inspired in all creatures of this world. Remind them that in those long nights at the end of the time we call the Copper-Rose Rain, there was an order of owls led by a brave king that rose to perform noble deeds and were joined by all manner of creatures both of land and air and sea who fought bravely, side by side, for the good of all.*

# OWLS
## *and others from the*
# GUARDIANS OF GA'HOOLE SERIES

### The Band

SOREN: Barn Owl, *Tyto alba,* from the Forest Kingdom of Tyto; escaped from St. Aegolius Academy for Orphaned Owls; a Guardian at the Great Ga'Hoole Tree and close advisor to the King

GYLFIE: Elf Owl, *Micranthene whitneyi,* from the desert kingdom of Kuneer; escaped from St. Aegolius Academy for Orphaned Owls; Soren's best friend; a Guardian at the Great Ga'Hoole Tree and ryb of the navigation chaw

TWILIGHT: Great Gray Owl, *Strix nebulosa,* free flier, orphaned within hours of hatching; Guardian at the Great Ga'Hoole Tree

DIGGER: Burrowing Owl, *Speotyto cunicularius,* from the desert kingdom of Kuneer; lost in desert after attack in which his brother was killed by owls from St. Aegolius; Guardian at the Great Ga'Hoole Tree

The Leaders of the Great Ga'Hoole Tree

CORYN: Barn Owl, *Tyto alba,* the young king of the great tree; son of Nyra, leader of the Pure Ones

EZYLRYB: Whiskered Screech Owl, *Otus trichopsis,* Soren's former mentor, the wise, much-loved, departed ryb at the great Ga'Hoole Tree

Others at the Great Ga'Hoole Tree

OTULISSA: Spotted Owl, *Strix occidentalis,* chief ryb and ryb of Ga'Hoolology and weather chaws; an owl of great learning and prestigious lineage

MARTIN: Northern Saw-whet Owl, *Aegolius acadicus,* member of the Chaw of Chaws; a Guardian at the Great Ga'Hoole Tree

RUBY: Short-eared Owl, *Asio flammeus,* member of the Chaw of Chaws; a Guardian at the Great Ga'Hoole Tree

EGLANTINE: Barn Owl, *Tyto alba,* Soren's younger sister

MADAME PLONK: Snowy Owl, *Nyctea scandiaca,* the elegant singer of the Great Ga'Hoole Tree

MRS. PLITHIVER: blind snake, formerly the nest-maid for Soren's family; now a member of the harp guild at the Great Ga'Hoole Tree

OCTAVIA: Kielian snake, nest-maid for many years for Madame Plonk and Ezylryb (also known as BRIGID)

DOC FINEBEAK: Snowy Owl, *Nyctea scandiaca,* famed freelance tracker once in the employ of the Pure Ones

## Characters from the Time of the Legends

GRANK: Spotted Owl, *Strix occidentalis,* the first collier; friend to young King H'rath and Queen Siv during their youth; first owl to find the ember

HOOLE: Spotted Owl, *Strix occidentalis,* son of H'rath; retriever of the Ember of Hoole; founder and first king of the great tree

H'RATH: Spotted Owl, *Strix occidentalis,* king of the N'yrthghar, the frigid region known in later times as the Northern Kingdoms; father of Hoole

SIV: Spotted Owl, *Strix occidentalis,* queen of H'rath of the N'yrthghar; mother of Hoole.

KREETH: Female hagsfiend with strong powers of nachtmagen; friend of Ygryk, conjured Lutta into being

## The Pure Ones

KLUDD: Barn Owl, *Tyto alba,* Soren's older brother, slain leader of the Pure Ones (also known as METAL BEAK and HIGH TYTO)

NYRA: Barn Owl, *Tyto alba,* Kludd's mate, leader of the Pure ones after Kludd's death

DUSTYTUFT: Greater Sooty Owl, *Tyto tenebricosa,* low-caste owl in the Pure ones, friend of Nyroc since his hatching (also known as PHILLIP)

UGLAMORE: Barn Owl, *Tyto alba,* a Pure Guard sublieutenant under Nyra who deserts the Pure Ones

TARN: Burrowing Owl, *Speotyto cunicularius,* a Pure One commander under Nyra and a brilliant tactician

Other Characters

DUNLEAVY MACHEATH: treacherous dire wolf, once leader of the MacHeath clan in Beyond the Beyond

GYLLBANE: courageous member of the MacHeath clan of dire wolves, her pup Cody died keeping the Book of Kreeth from the Pure Ones (also known as NAMARA)

BESS: Boreal Owl, *Aegolius funerus,* daughter of Grimble, a guard at St. Aegolius Academy for Orphaned Owls; keeper of the Palace of Mists (also known as THE KNOWER)

BRAITHE: Whiskered Screech Owl, *Otus trichopsis,* owl from Ambala and a memorizer of books; flew with the Greenowls of Ambala to the great tree on Balefire Night

CLEVE OF FIRTHMORE: Spotted Owl, *Striz accidentalis,* of the noble family of Krakor, healer, pacifist

Blue Owls

STRIGA: Blue Snowy Owl, *Nyctea scandiaca,* a former dragon owl from the Middle Kingdom seeking a more meaningful life (also known as ORLANDO)

TENGSHU: Blue Long-eared Owl, *Asio otis,* qui master and sage of the Middle Kingdom

# *Acknowledgments*

As in previous Guardians of Ga'Hoole books, I have taken much inspiration from history. In Chapter 15 the speech given by the H'ryth is based on one given by Winston Churchill in 1940 in the House of Commons during World War II.

The final battle in the War of the Ember is modeled after the famous battle of Thermopylae in the year 480 B.C., where the Spartan soldiers at a rocky mountain pass in northern Greece stood three hundred strong against the invading Persian army who outnumbered them many times over. When Nyra warns Coryn that his strategy will not work without the sun and Coryn replies, "Then we shall fight you in the shade," these are the same words that the warrior Dienekes replied to the threat delivered by the Persian king Xerxes as reported by Herodotus, the ancient Greek historian. Similarly in the epilogue of *The War of The Ember* when Otulissa begins to write the history of this great battle, one of the sentences in the last paragraph is an adaptation of the words of the fifth-century Greek lyric poet Simonides, words that can be found today on the memorial epitaph at the site of the battle of Thermopylae.

Being a writer is not really as lonely a job as many people might think. In the end, writing a book is truly a collaboration. I have acknowledged history and then people such as Winston Churchill, whose use of language I find profoundly moving. I have recognized my readers, who through their enthusiasm have sustained and stirred me to keeping writing more in this series. And now I must speak briefly of my four muses.

Ann Reit loved my idea for the Guardians of Ga'Hoole and is responsible for bringing it to the attention of the people at Scholastic who were so important in giving it the great launch.

Joy Peskin edited the first five books. I am so grateful to her for her unmitigated optimism when I often faced what I thought were insurmountable problems as we sought to establish an overall narrative arc for these first books.

Maria Weisbin, who edited the last ten books, has the most extraordinary editorial eye I have ever encountered in my thirty years of writing. Her ear for language, her sense of plot and pacing is simply unmatched. She is a woman of profound sensibilities, and her contribution to these books is beyond measure.

And finally there was, and is, the late Craig Walker, who was truly my Ezylryb. May he be ever happy in glaumora.

A peek at

THE GUARDIANS *of* GA'HOOLE

*Lost Tales of Ga'Hoole*

Greetings, Dear Readers!

I come to you not as a monarch, but as an old friend from the Great Ga'Hoole Tree. I write at Otulissa's request. She asks that I give you news of the tree and introduce the tales she has gathered. And so I shall.

It seems we have entered a time of blessed peace. The Striga and his vicious Blue Brigade fell in defeat many moon cycles ago. Nyra and the Pure Ones are gone. The dedication to learning fostered at the great tree has spread throughout the kingdoms, bringing with it the fresh breeze of knowledge and banishing the dank residue of ignorance, superstition, and malice. The arts of reading and even writing are no longer rare beyond the tree. Deep in the forest of Ambala, a simple printing press has been built with the help of the newly established research-and-printing chaw from the great tree, so that in that hidden dell where great works are chanted into the emerald air, they are now put down in printed scrolls and books as well. This new press, and our own press at the great tree, supply a small but growing number of lending libraries that have been established in the owl kingdoms, so that great works from the tree, from the Glauxian Brothers' and Glauxian Sisters' retreats, and from the library of the Others in the Palace of Mists, may be studied in distant dens and hollows by furred, scaled, and feathered scholars alike.

It is perhaps natural that in such times of outward peace, we look inward. And so it is that the personal and, in some cases, secret histories of our own Guardians and others close to the tree have now come to light. Otulissa has studied, researched, and sometimes simply listened with a wise and sympathetic ear slit, and set down the tales for all to learn from. As you read these tales of personal history, private anguish, and worldly adventure, remember that not all battles are fought in the air or on the ground. Some, perhaps the most difficult of all, are fought in our own gizzards, hearts, and brains.

I submit these tales to you with respect and affection.

Soren

Guardian Among Guardians